Fra

Stag Bro

By Lainey Davis

© 2018 Lainey Davis

Want to keep up with Lainey's new releases?
<u>Sign up for my newsletter</u> for a free story, exclusive content,
and more!
http://eepurl.com/dvDKzH

All rights reserved. No portion of this book may be
reproduced in any form without permission from the
publisher, except as permitted by U.S. copyright law.

This is a work of fiction. Names, characters, business, events
and incidents are the products of the author's imagination.
Any resemblance to actual persons, living or dead, or actual
events is purely coincidental.

Individuals pictured on the cover are models and are used for
illustrative purposes only.

Many thanks to Nicky Lewis, Mandy Dr., Christine,
Samantha, Keith G, and Judy for editorial input.

Thank you for supporting
independent authors!

Table of Contents

One
THATCHER

I realize the second I finish that I have no idea what this chick's name is. Did we talk about names? Or did we just walk back to her apartment last night? I don't usually stay over, but I was completely exhausted after our acrobatic routine in her living room, her hallway, and her bed. And then she was down for an encore this morning...so here I am.

"Fuck," I shout, looking at her clock radio. "Is that the right time?"

She rolls over, pushing the curtain of her blonde hair out of her eyes. "Mmmm. I guess so." She runs her fingers lightly along my chest, letting her head flop back down on the pillow.

"Fuck. I'm so fucking late. Shit." I'm out of the bed in a flash, scrambling around her apartment looking for my clothes. I'm going to have to go wearing the same stuff I had on last night. I run my fingers through my long hair, trying to tame it a little. My family is going to kill me.

"Thatcher, wait." I hear her padding down the hall, still naked. Fuck me, she's hot. A tall, leggy blonde with big eyes and full lips. Do I want to get her number? Fuck it.

"Babe, I'm sorry. I have to get out of here." I find my wallet under the couch near my jeans. My keys...aha! They're on the floor inside the front door. When I stand up with them I see her standing with her arms crossed.

She raises an eyebrow. "You're just going to run out of here like this? Literally run out?"

"It's my nephew's birthday party. I'm sorry. I didn't mean to--"

"Give me five minutes and I'll come with you."

Woah. "What?" My tone is harsh, but is she serious right now?

"Bring me with you. To the party. I love kids!"

I hold my hands out, palms up. "Look, doll, we just met last night. I don't want you to take this the wrong way, but I can't bring you with me to my nephew's birthday party with my family."

"Doll? Babe? You don't even know my name do you?"

I open my mouth and then close it again. Fuck it. I wasn't coming back for more anyway.

"Fuck you, Thatcher Stag. Fuck you!" She starts throwing magazines at me from the shelf in the hall. I duck as a huge bridal catalogue comes flying at my head and then I remember. "Amber!" I look at the address label from one of the projectiles. Fuck. "Tiffany, come on. You seemed like you had a good time..."

She shakes her head. "You are unbelievable."

I don't have time to talk about this more. My brother is going to tear me a new one if I'm not there for this party. I pull the door open and then shut, jogging a bit to find my beat up old Ford Ranger parked outside. I slam the truck into gear and screech out of the parking lot just as I see Tiffany stick her head out the apartment window. I don't even hear what she's shouting at me.

I take stock of myself. My hair and beard are a mess. There's definitely lipstick on the collar of my polo. I'll have to go in just my undershirt. I wonder if my brother will buy it if I say I got hung up in my work this morning and lost track of time.

Luckily I have my nephew's gift with me. I can tell them I was putting the finishing touches on it, even though I've had it done for months. I had picked it up from the engraver last night before I hit the club, which was why I had it along, tucked safely in the glove box.

I pull up outside my brother's house in Highland Park. It's the house we all grew up in, where Tim took care of us after my mom died and my dad took off. Now Tim lives here with his wife, Alice, and their baby. Tim's always been hard on us, insisting that we keep our shit together. And with good reason. It's not like it rained money for our family. We had to be careful, couldn't afford any missteps. But I'm an adult now, and Tim's become even more of a hard ass since he married Alice. At least with me.

Our other brother, Ty, can do no wrong as far as Tim's concerned. Ty is a professional hockey star and his fiancé, Juniper, is a lawyer at my brother's firm. She used to be Ty's lawyer until they got together. Tim acts like the sun shines out of Juniper's ass and Ty is basically another sunbeam, between all his community service and the way he helped Juniper train for an Olympic gold medal in rowing.

I'm left to bear the brunt of all of them judging me. They think I'm some dirty, deadbeat, wanna-be artist. They think I'm a selfish womanizer, and maybe that part is true. I breathe slowly in and out through my nose. *Yeah. That part is true.*

I climb out of the truck and head inside, wondering how much I've missed and how long Tim is going to yell at me about it later.

Two
THATCHER

"Happy birthday, dear Peter, happy birthday to you!" I walk in the door in time to join the chorus singing to my nephew. I slide over to the dining room, where my family and Alice's family are all clapping and cooing at my nephew. He's strapped in his high chair wearing just a diaper as my sister-in-law slides him a giant cupcake. She's a chef, so I'm sure she made it for him from scratch. Knowing Alice, it's probably made of carrot flour with lemon zest and extra protein or some shit...but tastes amazing anyway.

I pull out my phone and take a picture as Petey smacks the chocolate frosting, then rubs his hand on his belly. He's a cute kid, with his mom's tight, blond ringlets but the grey eyes all us Stag men inherited from our mother, Laurel. Petey sticks a hand in his mouth, tentative, and then the sugary icing blows his little mind. He dives in, face first. We all laugh, but when I look up, I see my brother Tim scowling at me.

I raise both my eyebrows at Tim, but don't keep his eye. I look back at Petey. He's got, like, 15 adults staring at him and his cousins--Alice's sister has 2 boys--are running around screaming. The poor kid must be going crazy with all the stimulation, plus his first experience with sugar.

"All right, Petey, let's get you cleaned up and we can open your presents!" Alice swoops in and lifts him out of the chair, not even flinching at the mess. She's like that. Doesn't care about stuff like frosting on her shirt. She holds Petey on her hip, trying to keep most of the mess at bay. He reaches for her face and she kisses his chocolaty hand. I take a picture of that, too. Alice has brought a lot of light into our family.

Things were really rocky with Tim and her for a bit there. She got pregnant pretty early in their relationship and insisted she had to raise the baby within walking distance of her family. Tim wanted them to live in the fancy downtown penthouse he owned at the time. Alice would have none of it. Family is the most important thing to her, and I appreciate that. I mean, my brothers are pains in the ass, but they're all I've got. The Petersons are way up in each other's business--a few of them still live at home with their dad and Alice's older brother just bought a house in the neighborhood. I laugh a little at how nicely things worked out now that Alice and Tim live in Stag HQ. Alice grew up just a few blocks away from us. We're all one, giant Stag-Peterson group now for Sunday dinners and shit. It's nice. At least Alice's brothers don't judge me for my piercings and ink.

I meet Tim's eye again as Alice and her sister get Peter started opening presents. Yep. Tim is pissed. I shift uncomfortably, grabbing a plate of snacks off the table while

Fragile Illusion

Petey opens toy cars and a tricycle. Of course, Ty bought him a hockey stick and Juniper got him a life jacket.

I crouch down next to Alice and Peter to give him my gift. Alice sniffs and makes a face at me. *Shit.* How bad do I stink? I need to start keeping deodorant in the truck, at least. I slide the wooden box out of my back jeans pocket and hand it to Alice. "I made something for you, dude." Peter smiles at me and tugs at my beard. He's the only one I'll let do that. I know it's wild and unruly, but that doesn't give anyone free reign to yank it. Except Petey.

"Thatcher, this box is gorgeous," Alice says, rubbing the smooth finish.

"My buddy made that for me, and engraved it. See?" I point out where Property of Peter Stag is etched into the wood. She hands me the box and I show her how to slide the lid open. The glass marbles I made glisten in the light.

"Marbles, Thatcher? For a baby?" My brother is angry. He's about to blow his shit, I can tell. He storms over and snatches them from Alice's hand.

"Chill, dude. I used the silicon blend for the base material." I take a marble from him and bounce it on the hardwood floor. "It won't shatter. He can't break it. I promise."

"It's a fucking choking hazard, Thatcher." Tim takes the box and moves to put it up on top of the bookshelf, but I grab his arm.

Lainey Davis

"Give me a little more credit than that, would you?" I hold up one of the marbles. "Alice told me nothing smaller than a toilet paper roll. I made sure these were *just* bigger." I look back and forth between Tim and Alice. She smiles at me warmly, but my brother clenches his teeth. I see a vein ticking in his neck and he walks through to the kitchen.

"Thatcher, they're just beautiful," Alice says. She holds one of the marbles up to the light. I swirled in black and gold on that one, for our Pittsburgh sports teams. The other marble I made with grey, like our eyes. And a few streaks of purple, for Alice's. I'm pretty pleased with how they turned out. Perfectly spherical. Lightweight enough that I don't worry Petey will hurt himself with them. I know I'm an asshole to women and I show up late to birthday parties, but I would never give my nephew a gift that would hurt him. My family is everything to me.

Alice kisses me on the cheek. "Go talk to him," she urges. "He's just being cranky, I think."

I nod and grab a cupcake before the kids and Ty eat them all. I sigh and walk to the kitchen, where Tim is gripping the counter and staring out the window into the backyard. "Hey, Timber," I say, my mouth full of cupcake.

"You're a real piece of work, you know that, Thatcher?"

"Dude, I was a half hour late for a baby's birthday party. Can you cut me a break?" I wipe my mouth with the back of

Fragile Illusion

my hand. "And at least turn around to look at me if you're going to give me shit."

Tim whips around and crosses his arms, talking to me like I'm some little kid. "You still smell like pussy. Do you know that? And fucking liquor, too. Did you even shower after?"

I don't say anything, but I don't think it can be true that I reek that badly of sex...although I did go down on what's-her-name in my truck before we headed to her apartment.

"What do you care what I did last night?"

"I care when you show up hungover and dripping with STDs to my son's fucking birthday party, Thatcher. You're late for every family dinner. You're always out at bars. What the fuck are you doing with your life?"

I throw the rest of the cupcake into the sink. "You have a lot of fucking nerve, Tim, judging my life. I go to functions promoting my god damn artwork and it's really none of your fucking business who I bring home."

"It is my business, brother." He steps right into my face. "It is my business when you bring some bimbo to the family suite to watch Ty's hockey games and then you piss her the fuck off and she slanders the family name on social media. It is my business when you screw over some executive's daughter and I start losing business to other firms. Are you sensing a pattern here?" He holds up his phone and I see

Tiffany has been bashing me online already. That didn't take long.

"Her father represents the football team, Thatcher," Tim snarls at me. "I've already gotten calls." He grinds his teeth together and I can tell he wants to deck me or sue me. Maybe both.

The thing about Tim is that he's 100% correct about me pissing off all these women. Yeah, I go to my brother Ty's pro hockey games and seduce the glamorous women there, and yeah. I forget their names, sneak out of their beds in the middle of the night, or wind up fucking their roommates the next weekend. But they all know this going in. They all know that Thatcher Stag isn't in it for the long haul. One great night. I make it worth their while.

The other thing about Tim is that he's 100% an asshole right now, and I just can't stand it another fucking second. He's always harping on me for how I do business, because it's not how *he* does business at Stag Law. Fuck him and his uptight, designer suits. He has no idea how successful I am, the kinds of negotiations my agent makes for my glass. Could I be a bit more discreet about how I unwind after work? Ok, maybe.

But my whole life, he's just treated me like his whipping boy, taking out all his frustrations on me because Ty's the youngest and I'm always just *there*. But I'm sick of him thinking of me as a loser, which is why I respond to him by saying, "I don't know where you get your information from, Tim, but it's outdated. And that chick is delusional. I'll have you know I'm engaged."

I hear a gasp from behind me. Alice and Juniper had walked into the kitchen to see what the commotion was as Tim and I were shouting. Juniper claps her hands. "Engaged? Thatcher, really?? Why didn't you say anything?"

"Yeah, brother. Why didn't you tell us anything about this fiancé of yours?" Tim raises an eyebrow at me and I can tell he knows I'm lying. Fuck him.

I run a finger through my long hair, trying to smooth it down. "I didn't want to take away from your wedding plans, Juniper. This summer is about you and Ty and I don't want to steal your limelight is all."

"Aww, Thatcher, you are so sweet to consider me that way. You know you getting engaged wouldn't take anything from my wedding, though."

I give her a 2-dimple smile. Not that she can see them behind the beard. "I just know you don't have any family, Juniper, so *our* family should dote on you. This is a big deal for you. You guys can all meet her soon. I promise."

Tim is looking at me like he still wants to murder me. "Why didn't you bring her with you today, then, if she's your fiancé?"

I shrug, stalling. "She's working." Shit. I need to start keeping track of the lies before I get myself in trouble. I just want to get my brother off my back for a minute so I can regroup.

"Well!" Alice throws her arms around me in a hug. "I insist that you bring her over for family dinner next Sunday. No-- Thatcher, don't you look at me that way. She has to come. Tell her to ask off now if she works weekends."

My mouth drops open. I look at Tim and he's smiling like the Cheshire cat. "Great idea, Alice. I need to meet this mystery woman so I can call Tiffany's father and assure him his daughter must have been thinking of a different hipster artist who fucked her and forgot her name."

I'm seething right now, angry...and panicking, I guess. I can't fucking bear to let him be right about this. "We will be here, brother. Count on it."

I guess I have a week to find myself a fake fiancé.

Three
EMMA

I smooth out my jeans and tie my hair up in a high ponytail to get it out of my face. I've been summoned to the editor's office, but I'm wearing my "thinking clothes" and I look a mess. I tap on Phil's door frame hesitantly. "You wanted to see me, boss?" He gestures for me to come in, so I sit in the chair by his desk while he types furiously. Hopefully those aren't comments on my latest draft. He has high standards, and I want to improve my writing, but it's still hard to get a file back that's more red ink than black.

Phil stops typing, sighs, and leans back in his chair. "Emma. I need you to do something for me."

"Sure, Phil. Anything for the Post!"

He sighs again. "Davis quit and, frankly, I'm screwed. I need you to cover an art opening."

Art? I frown. "Hm. Well, Phil, you know I don't really know anything about art..."

He waves a hand, dismissing this concern. "I'm emailing you all the press release stuff. You can pick up lingo, highlights, whatever from the PR people. Thatcher Stag is debuting some series of glass botanicals in the conservatory. It's supposed to be hot shit. We need to cover it." He looks at me over his monitor, face stern. "Consider it an advertorial--

think positive copy, Cheswick. Ben will go photograph the event. You just need to interview the artist, get some quotes about his process and his vision for our city. Blah, blah. You realize I'm giving you *permission* to write a puff piece here, Cheswick."

My frown deepens. This job as a general reporter at the Pittsburgh Post is a dream for me. Only because I pushed myself so hard in college did I have a strong enough portfolio to land a job here at all, and then I got promoted to reporter. For the past six months I've been writing whatever Phil tells me to write, whether that's meant interviewing city council or watching kids race robots around the science center. But art? I'm not an artsy gal.

"Davis really quit? Can we just expand our coverage of local science initiatives?"

"Emma, we've got investors. Surely you've noticed that we have an arts and culture section? I'm assuming you read every issue cover to cover?" I blush. He smiles. "You will write me 2,000 words on Thatcher Stag's glass show, and you will submit your copy by end of work day tomorrow." I open my mouth to protest, but he holds up his hand. "Go home, change into something more presentable, and be at the conservatory by 5."

He throws me my press credentials and a parking pass he knows I don't need, because I don't drive. *Fifteen years of uncontrolled seizures took away that opportunity,* I think, letting myself feel angry for just a moment before I shake it off. I've been healthy for over four years. I'm in a good place now. I pick at the medical alert bracelet on my wrist as I head back to my cubicle and grab my things from my desk.

I walk the few short blocks home, thankful as always that I got a job in such a walkable neighborhood. I cut through the park, trying to plan out questions to ask an artist about his work. God, I really know *nothing* about art. I smile despite it all when I reach my apartment. I'm able to afford the first floor of an airy duplex on the north side of the city, where I got a good deal by promising to help the landlord write ads for her vacant apartments. Now she doesn't have any vacancies, and I've got cheap rent in an amazing space. The beautiful brick building was lovingly restored with gorgeous woodwork, wide plank hardwood floors throughout, and large windows that let in tons of sunlight. I put two huge planters of lavender and sage on my stoop, since they do so well in the direct sun, and the place looks inviting. Like a real adult lives here. *I am an independent adult, and I'm doing great,* I remind myself. It still takes me by surprise sometimes.

My parents won't even come visit. They insist this neighborhood is "unsuitable" and I can tell they disapprove of my job as a reporter. I'm sure they'd be much happier if I had pursued political science like my perfect sister Veronica. I shake my head, trying not to think too much about my parents, and investigate my wardrobe options.

I ordinarily wear all black when I'm working, but it's a hot day and Phil didn't specify whether the exhibit would be indoors or out. I settle on black slacks with a lightweight grey top with a boatneck cut and 3/4 sleeves. It's a bit more snug than my typical reporting getup, but I remind myself that just because something fits doesn't mean it's inappropriate. My mother's rules about modesty and proper dress always baffled me. I spent years with her cramming me into pencil skirts and "respectable nude pumps." I cringe just thinking about it as I slide my feet into my favorite flats.

Since college, I've relied on my friend Nicole to coach me through most decisions that don't involve pearls and formal dinners. If Nicole said this top was ok for work, it must be true. She's working for a tech startup, but always looks like she could be featured in our Lifestyles section in the Post.

When I arrive at the venue, my breath catches. The gardens are so lush, so serene. I can't believe I haven't come here since I was a kid. I giggle, imagining my mother here for a fancy hat party, and I flash my press pass at the entrance. As I walk up the main stairs, I almost trip while staring up at the glass chandelier. Brilliant curls of glass in green, blue, and yellow intertwine, catching the light of the glass dome entryway. When the automatic doors slide open to reveal the

Fragile Illusion

exhibit, I am thrilled by the floral scent, the dazzling green plants, and the fiery shoots of glass I see peeking out from among the leaves. Maybe this won't be so bad of an assignment.

Spotting someone wearing a lanyard, I step into his path. "Excuse me," I say. "I'm Emma Cheswick from the *Pittsburgh Post*. I'm here to talk to Thatcher Stag. Would you be able to point him out to me?"

The man grins. He waggles his eyebrows, which seems strange to me, and he yells across the room toward a long-haired man squatting by an orange piece of glass. "Yo, Thatch. This chick is here to talk to you." My face twists in confused anger at this misrepresentation, but before I can elaborate, the strange guy brushes past and the man who must be Thatcher walks over.

He's wearing stained jeans that hang from his hips in such a way that I can see he has a perfect, round ass. His ripped t-shirt barely hides the black ink twined around his muscular arms. Shit, he's hot. *Remember, he's a subject. Not a conquest.* Thatcher leans on a column and crosses his arms, smiling at me. "The show opens in about an hour, sweetheart, but we've probably got time for a decent *conversation."*

Is he hitting on me? I hold out a hand for a shake. "Emma Cheswick. *Pittsburgh Post.* I'm actually--"

"Emma. I like that. Follow me and we can *talk* back in one of the offices." He winks, and walks in front of me, holding back a palm frond for me as we head through a side door in the conservatory. "So how'd you get in early, Emma? The ladies usually come find me *after* the show..."

I'm feeling less and less interested in this guy the more he talks. "I just waved my press pass. It hadn't occurred to me to look for you afterward. I guess that makes sense--what the hell??"

Thatcher spins me around so my back presses against a wall in the hall. Boxing me in with both arms, he leans in close. He smells like sweat and fire. And he definitely is hitting on me. I stiffen. "What, baby? You shy about being in the hallway?" He raises a hand to, I think, stroke my cheek, but I duck out from under his arm.

"You know what? I can get what I need from the conservatory PR people. Have a good show, Mr. Stag." I rush back out the door and into the atrium before he can formulate a response.

Four
EMMA

I walk away from him as quickly as I can, digging in my bag for my phone. I text Phil. **Thatcher Stag is a sleazeball. He just made a pass at me.**

My editor responds almost immediately. *All men are assholes. Find someone from the conservatory to help you. Get this interview, Cheswick.*

Unbelievable. I bite my lip and tap my foot, trying to figure out what to do next. I decide to just start wandering the space before the crowd arrives. As I walk through the purple and pink orchids, I see more of what must be Thatcher's art. His glass is delicate and ferocious at once. The contrast to the green surrounding it is stark, and yet I can tell each piece was placed intentionally, toughtfully. His work is not so different from the flowers in the room. Some of the orchids sprout seemingly from nothing--no roots or dirt to be seen. His glass seems more natural here than those delicate, outlandish blooms. How can one man create something so beautiful and also be such a jerk?

When I've made a full lap of the inside, I've sufficiently calmed down to go searching for the PR staff from the conservatory. A smiling woman named Linda shakes my hand warmly and hands me a whole packet of information about the exhibit, the flowers that accompany it, and the conservatory's vision in hiring a glass artist to embellish their space.

"Anything else I can help you with, Emma? You know we're always thrilled for page space in the Post."

"Well," I say. "Actually...about Thatcher..."

Her face falls. "Yes. About Thatcher."

"I need to get a few quotes from him, but he seemed...distracted when I tried to speak with him earlier."

Linda rolls her eyes. "Will you be here for awhile? Do you want to give me your questions and I can make sure he answers them? I've got an intern who can record him talking while he...finishes setting up."

"Oh! That's a perfect solution." I mean, it's not. Third-hand interviews are a terrible idea, but Phil did say it was a puff piece, and I did tell him the source was a dick. So I tear my question list from my notebook and hand it to Linda. "I'll just interview some of the guests about their feelings when they experience the exhibit and I'll make sure I find you before I leave?"

Linda nods and marches off. I see her hand over the slip of paper before embracing someone from Pittsburgh Magazine. I wander through the garden, chatting with people about the glass and the flowers. An hour or so later, I've almost forgotten that Thatcher Stag lured me into a hallway and tried to make out with me. Almost.

I finish up my conversation with a middle-aged woman named Marge, who drove in from south of the city to enjoy the show. She's got me answering questions about growing up in the same suburban town where she lives, and when I see Thatcher approaching us, it takes me a real minute to figure out which scenario is less annoying.

He sidles up to us, snagging two glasses of champagne from a server standing nearby. "May I offer you ladies a drink?" he says, smiling a crooked grin that only raises one side of his mouth. Why am I looking at his straight, white teeth? Maybe because I want to punch them out, I decide.

I shake my head at his offer. "No, thank you. I'm on the clock. Marge was telling me how much she's enjoying your art, though."

Marge is delighted. "Oh are *you* Thatcher Stag?? This Stag Glass show is simply superb." She flutters a hand to her chest and takes a flute of champagne from Thatcher. I smirk at him and duck away. Seeing Linda glide past, I rush over to her.

"I see you've got him distracted," she says as she hands me a thumb drive and my question sheet, where the intern has scribbled a few mono-syllabic answers to my carefully crafted questions. "Anyway. I think we've got about seven or eight words from him...his contact information is in the packet I

Lainey Davis

gave you if your fact checker wants to verify any quotes you can garner from that file."

"Thanks for trying, Linda. I appreciate you looking out for me." I assure her that I will talk to Phil and come back sometime to write an in-depth piece on the conservatory and their efforts to revitalize and attract more guests. "Phil loves when I find him good tourism leads," I assure her.

I head for home, frustrated and pissed off at my editor, Thatcher Stag, and anyone else I happen to encounter as I go. I send Nicole a series of furious texts and she sends me angry GIFs. *I can't believe your boss still wanted you to interview that scumbag after you told him he hit on you. I'll never buy Stag's bullshit tchotchkes.*

Thank you! You're a true friend.

In the morning, I sulk my way into work and bang out the meanest review I can tactfully write about the show and submit it to my editor before he leaves for lunch. Not ten minutes later, his admin pokes her head over my cubicle wall.

"Hey, Emma," she says, grimacing.

"That bad?" I sigh and start to stand.

"Phil wants to see you right away."

Five

THATCHER

After my installation opening, I decide to just go home. I can't get my fight with my brother out of my head and I'm very aware the clock is ticking for me to find someone to agree to fool my family for a few weeks until after Ty's wedding. There has to be someone who isn't mad at me after we hooked up...

My assistant, Cody, comes back with me for a few beers. I decide to let him know what's going on to see if he knows anyone who can play a role for a while.

"Dude, you rolled up to your nephew's birthday party right from a one-night stand? That's crude, man." Cody takes a deep pull on his beer. "Hm. I honestly can't think of a woman you haven't already fucked. You even fuck all their roommates...you're pretty prolific."

I throw my beer cap at him. "There has to be someone. Someone left from art school? One of the new grad students at the Pittsburgh Glass Center?"

Cody rubs a hand across his chin, thinking. "Hey, what about that reporter chick from tonight?"

"What reporter?"

Cody's eyes go wide. "The redhead chick who came early to interview you."

"That fucking girl was a reporter? You made her sound like some groupie." I stand up and my stool tips over backward. "Fuck, Cody, I made a move on her. What paper was she with?" *Don't say the Post.*

Cody thinks for a minute and my heart sinks when he says, "She was there from the Post. You hit on her? Really?"

"You called her a 'chick' and said she was there to talk to me."

"Yeah. For the paper." Cody swigs down the rest of his beer and throws his bottle into the bin by the workbench. "Look, Thatch, it's late. I'm going to get on out of here. I'll be in--what? Thursday morning?"

I'm so pissed off I can only nod. What the fuck is wrong with me? I don't even ask first anymore. I mean, to be fair, 90 per cent of the women who want to talk to me are using 'talk' as a euphemism. It's just my luck that the one woman who actually wanted to talk was a fucking reporter.

That opening was a really big deal for me. I never did anything like that before, partnering with a conservatory. I worked for months with them, talking about the different plants that would be in bloom when the show opened, discussing different pieces to highlight at different times of day to catch the light. One day I was in there at sunrise taking pictures, sketching out my ideas. It kills me to think the work won't even get a fair review because I can't turn off...whatever it is that makes me do that shit with women.

I'll just have to kiss her ass before she turns in her draft. I look around my shelf of finished work and my eye settles on a bonsai. At least, it was supposed to be a bonsai. It never looked quite right to me, so I set it aside. But it's beautiful-- clear roots and branches tipped with blues and blacks. I decide it will make a fine token of my apology.

In the morning, I shower slowly after a long run, making sure to condition my beard, comb my hair. I decide an apology calls for extra attention to how I look. I even stick a blazer on over my t-shirt. Apparently I needed a wakeup call to remember my manners. I've decided to drive into the Post, find whichever reporter I mauled, and offer my most sincere apology.

The sweet thing at reception is putty in my hands when I turn on the charm. I offer her my best smile--the one I save for when I really have to work for it with the ladies. I lean across the counter and check out her nametag. "Hey there, Mindy." My voice is smooth. I know I look good, smell good, and sound good. "I'm Thatcher Stag. Last night I got interrupted when one of your reporters was interviewing me at my art show, and I never got her card. Do you know how I could find her? Just to see if she had any more questions?"

"Last night? Gosh. Hm. It could have been anyone..." Mindy crinkles her nose and looks at a computer screen. "It was an art show? What did she look like?"

"She had red hair and green eyes," I say. "Maybe...this tall?" I hold my hand about mid-chest.

"Oh. That's Emma." Mindy sits back in her chair and looks down the hall. "She got called in to talk to Phil, though. I actually think she will be glad you're here." She stands and walks around the desk, nodding toward the doorway. "Come on. I'll take you back."

I can hear shouting from halfway down the hall. Mindy points to the door that says EDITOR and heads back up front to the desk. I give her a wink and move closer to the editor's office, and I hear someone shouting my name from inside.

"Jesus, Cheswick. Did you even fucking Google him? I told you I wanted a puff piece. I absolutely cannot print a scathing defamation of his character."

Then I hear a familiar voice, sounding about as angry as she was last night. "Nothing I wrote there is untrue. He *is* a smarmy creep, and I did talk about how his delicate glass pieces brought light to the conservatory, in contrast to his awful personality."

I hear someone pound on the desk. "Damn it, Emma. Do you know who owns this paper?"

"Lash? What's that got to do with anything?"

The editor sighs. "Do you know who represents Lash, legally? Who is a major donor to our paper and likely funds the majority of your entry-level reporter salary?" He waits a beat. "Tim Stag. Older brother of Thatcher Stag, who I told you to write a fucking puff piece about."

"Phil, that feels inappropriate."

"It's not above the fold on the front page, Emma. It's Arts and Culture. If I wanted an exposé on Stag as a womanizer, I'd send you out to report the hell out of that story. But I want a nice, glowing review of the art show. Did you look at the art? Did you read the PR materials? Ok, then. Get the hell out of here and don't come back until you've got something I can work with. And get me a fucking quote!"

I can't help but smile, even if I am irritated that my brother's name gets evoked whenever I try to do anything. Emma's going to have to talk to me. When the office door flies open I lean back against the opposite wall, holding out my olive branch. She growls when she sees me standing there and her eyes fly wide open. "What the hell are you doing here?" She practically hisses at me.

"Sounds like I'm saving your ass, sweetheart."

Six

EMMA

I drag Thatcher Stag through the office by the lapels of his blazer, only partially wondering why he's more dressed up today to come to the Post's headquarters than he was at his damn art opening. Once we reach the lobby, I let go of him and start laying into him. "Look, I don't know what you heard or what you are thinking, but you can't be here right now. I'd prefer if you left."

The asshole grins at me. "From what I heard, your boss wants you talking to me. Pronto. Asking me in depth questions. Sounds like it could take hours..."

I can only roll my eyes. Because of course he's right. I stomp my foot in frustration. I need to talk to this dickhead. *At least he smells amazing,* I think, immediately angry at myself for noticing. "Look," I say, "there's no place here to do an interview and I'd feel safer speaking with you in a public place. Can you meet me in the library on Federal in a half hour?"

"No." He smiles.

"What do you mean 'no'? I thought you just said you were here to talk to me."

"I've got conditions," he says.

I raise an eyebrow and cross my arms. "I'm absolutely not sleeping with you, so you can get that out of your head right the hell now."

He laughs. "Nothing like that, doll. I do need a favor, though."

I glance over at reception to see if Mindy is listening. Of course she is. Thatcher notices this, too, and says, "Walk me to my truck and I'll tell you what I have in mind."

I think about it for a few minutes, while watching him grow visibly uncomfortable. Before I open my mouth to talk again, he holds out a cardboard box. "I brought you something," he says. "By way of apology for my behavior last night."

Well, this is unexpected. "Thank you," I say. I crack open the box, peering past the lid, and then I gasp as I pull out a glass cluster of neurons. The work is exquisite, delicate. The bundle of nerve endings splays out blue and black from the stem in the middle. This is exactly how I always imagined things looked inside me. Exactly! How could he possibly know to give this to me? "Who told you about me?" My voice quivers more than I intended, and his face softens.

"Nobody said anything about you, Emma. I just thought you'd like this enough to accept my apology and hear me out. So will you walk with me a minute?" He rubs a hand through his beard, nervously.

I can only nod, tucking the glass back into the box. "Can I go stick this on my desk? I don't want to drop it and break it."

"So you like it then?" He raises his eyebrows, hopeful, and I can't help but smile. He looks like a kid who just made something for his parents. It's endearing to me that he cares whether I like his art.

My voice is a whisper when I tell him, "I love it, Thatcher." I rush off down the hall and slide the box across my desk. I grab my messenger bag and shove my laptop and digital recorder inside. I nod toward the doors and Thatcher walks with me.

Once we're outside, he leans against a battered old truck and says, "So here's the thing." He runs his hands through his beard again. "I'm in some deep shit with my family...and I'm just going to cut right to the chase. I need someone to pretend she's my fiancé until after my brother's wedding."

I wait a beat for him to laugh, tell me he's joking. Get to the real favor. He doesn't. "So...what now? You want me to *pretend* I'm going to marry you?"

He nods. "I promise I will give you unfettered access to me, and my studio, and I'll answer your questions without cracking jokes. You show up to, like, 2 family dinners with me and be my date for my brother's wedding and we'll call it even."

"Are you serious right now? That plan is absurd. And besides, a month of acting like I can tolerate you is way more effort than you answering my questions about glass in the gardens."

Now the mischievous grin returns and I feel myself wanting to slug him again. "It doesn't sound like your boss will like it very much if I clam up and refuse to talk to you."

Shit. He's right. I'm in deep trouble with Phil. He made that pretty clear in his office. I exhale slowly through my nose and Thatcher just stares at me, like he's studying me, and it makes me uncomfortable.

"I'll tell you what," he says. "I'll get you an in for another story that would be great for the Post, and I'll make sure you're the only reporter with access."

"What story is that," I ask, chewing on the inside of my cheek. He tells me that the woman his brother is going to marry is an Olympic gold medalist for rowing and that she has helped shift the mission of his *other* brother's law firm. "How many Stag brothers are there?" I ask, trying to keep it all straight. He grins and holds up 3 fingers.

"Tim is the oldest and runs Stag Law, which represents professional athletes *and* helps fight for equity for women in athletics, the arts...anywhere that gets federal Title 9 funds. And if you want to know more you'll have to agree to help me and talk with Juniper, because that is all I understand about what she does." He sticks his thumbs in his belt loops, looking like he's none too comfortable. What he's proposing sounds absolutely crazy...but he's right that I need this story. And it sounds like this pitch about his sister in law would be amazing to research and write.

I sigh, letting the air and frustration out of my entire body, and groan. "All right, Stag. I'll do it."

"Oh thank god," he says, visibly relaxing. He hands me his card with the address for his studio. We make a plan to meet there a bit later, and I text Phil that I'll have the revision for him tomorrow. Thatcher says we can hammer out the details for our pretend engagement over dinner later, and I agree to let him buy.

"But I am *not* sleeping with you. We need to clear that up right away."

He laughs. "I promise I will be on my best behavior." He opens the door to his truck and swings in, then rolls down the window and leans out halfway. "Unless you *want* me to misbehave." He winks, and I wish I had something to throw at him. But my imagination also flashes to images of Thatcher misbehaving with me, and I feel a flutter in my tummy.

"Get the hell out of here," I yell after him as he peals out, laughing. This is going to be a long month.

Fragile Illusion

<u>Seven</u>
THATCHER

I make an attempt to clean up my studio a bit before Emma gets here. I know she's supposed to write about me in a positive light no matter what, but I've never had anyone from the press meet me in my space before. I really don't let anyone in here but staff. My work in progress is too important to me, too private. I hope Emma doesn't look too carefully at the things that aren't complete. She seemed to really like the bonsai, though, so that sets my mind at ease a bit.

I start to think about why it matters to me that she likes my art. *That's different.* I usually don't give a shit what people think of my glass...buy it or move over has always been my motto. I feel bad for hitting on her at the conservatory. I guess I have to re-classify her as someone I know professionally. For some reason I'm always able to rein it in with women in a professional context. I could kill Cody for making me think she was a groupie. This whole thing could have been avoided.

It would be nice if she wants to get wild with me, though. I remember the way her body looked in those slim pants and that breezy top that gave just a hint of her curves. And fuck me, a red head. Even her eyelashes are red. I noticed when I was staring at her in the parking lot, pleading with her to accept my crazy scheme. I wonder what it feels like to wrap that red hair around my fist, yank her head back...suck on her neck. *Knock it off, Thatcher.* This is going to be a long month.

I've got to not only *not* hit on Emma, but I can't go out and find anyone else to sleep with, either. If word gets back to my family that I'm cheating on my so-called fiancé, Tim would treat me like worse garbage than he is already. It fucking sucks having perfect brothers.

I hear a knock at the door, and walk over to answer it a little too quickly. I curse under my breath when I see that it's not Emma Cheswick, but my sister in law Alice, blowing on my nephew's cheeks. Fuck. I totally forgot I told them I'd babysit tonight.

"And there's Uncle Thatcher!" Alice coos to Peter, who claps his hand and reaches for my beard. Always with the damn beard. I hope he doesn't have anything sticky on his fingers.

"Come here, squirt." I pull him in and toss him up on my shoulders, where he moves his hands immediately to my hair.

"Thatcher, I really appreciate you watching him for us tonight. It means so much to us to be able to go to Dad's retirement dinner." Her eyes shine. I know she's proud of her dad, and also feeling a little blue that her mom can't be here for this. Alice's mom died of cancer when she was in high school, just a few years after our mom died.

"Dude-time with Petey is my pleasure, Alice." I lean down so she can reach me to kiss my cheek. Her hair is wild and curly as ever, but I notice Petey doesn't yank on it like he does mine.

"My brother isn't with you is he," I ask, not sure what I hope the answer will be.

She shakes her head, though, and I feel some relief. "He's still at the office reviewing notes with Juniper. They're trying to get things squared away before she and Ty leave for their honeymoon. Tim's meeting me at the restaurant."

I nod. "Well, I want you both to have a great time and not worry. Whatever I can't figure out, I'll just Google." She bites her lower lip and creases her brow. "Relax, Alice. I've watched Peter before." I don't tell her that Emma will be here soon helping me out. That's what a fiancé does, right? Helps with the nephews. As Alice pulls away I smile, thinking this month might not be so bad after all.

Peter and I head into my attached apartment and I turn some kids show on the TV. I sit on the floor next to him to watch and he crawls right into my lap. I don't get a lot of one on one time with him. It's nice just chilling with the little dude, even if he does yank on my hair. Twenty minutes later, the doorbell rings. Emma.

I answer the door carrying Petey in a football hold, and he drools and laughs as Emma's face registers shock at seeing me with a baby.

"You have a *child?*"

"Ha! No way, babe. Petey here is my nephew and I forgot that we are hanging out tonight. Hope it's ok if he sits in on the interview."

Emma looks uncertain, but I step back from the door and Petey starts clapping his hands. He's damn charming, like all the Stag men. She can't help but smile, and we all sit together on the rug. "Fire away, Ms. Cheswick," I say, pulling Petey back from her laptop as she tries to open up all her stuff.

"Maybe I should sit up higher," she says, climbing onto the couch. Peter pulls himself to standing and slaps at her laptop. I like this kid even more. He's pushing Emma's buttons, literally, and she's cute as hell when she's irritated. Her face flushes as red as her hair.

I lie on my back on the carpet and start to play airplane with Peter so he's out of reach of Emma. "Thanks," she says, and I catch her staring at my abs as my t-shirt rides up when I swoop Petey around. "So, um, why don't you tell me how you first got interested in glass."

Eight
EMMA

I am shocked at how good Thatcher is with his nephew. He's so comfortable tossing that baby around. It's damn sexy, and I almost forget the man is a sleaze just looking for sex. When he tells me about how he feels like the molten glass is part of his mind, malleable and able to bring his imagination to solid form...well. It's easy to see why women drop their undies for him. He orders takeout, and we pig out on Indian food while he holds his end of the bargain. Thatcher Stag tells me how the art teachers at his school were his saving grace after his mom died, how they arranged for him to do intensive programs and helped him apply for a scholarship when he decided to study glass blowing in college. "Only Stag to leave the state for college," he says, laughing at how the tiny town of Alfred in New York never stood a chance against his artistic vision...or his libido.

Thatcher talks to me about his work for a while and then he looks at his watch. "Hey," he says, handing Petey a pouch of some sort of food. "My sister in law will be back soon to grab Petey, so we better hash out our plan. Basically, you need to act believably in love with me when my family's around."

"Ok." I chew on my pen. "How did we meet?"

He grins one of those devilish smiles I've come to recognize. He saves those for women he's trying to hit on. "You interviewed me at an opening," he says, "and you were smitten immediately."

"I'd prefer if *you* were the smitten one and had to work for it a bit," I tell him, and he nods.

"That sounds more plausible. All right, I can just tell my family I was smitten and drove to your office to give you a glass bonsai in an attempt to woo you. Then, you were smitten."

"That was a bonsai?" I think back to the beautiful cluster of neurons I now have on the mantle of my apartment, where it catches the afternoon sun just right and sparkles.

"Well yeah," he looks insulted. "What the hell did you think it was?"

I flush, not meaning to. Of course I hadn't meant to insult his art, but I am taken aback. I thought the gift was so personal to me. That he somehow knew about me and was, I don't know, honoring that by giving me a symbolic artistic creation. "I, um..." I decide I'm just going to be honest. I'm going to have to spend a lot of time with him for the next month and I will be lying to enough people as it is. "I thought it was a bundle of neurons."

He scrunches up his face as if he's thinking about this. "I can see that. The trunk was sort of messed up."

"I really like it, Thatcher." My voice comes out as a whisper. "I like it very much. Thank you again."

"You're welcome, Chezz." We start to talk about the family dinner I will need to attend on Sunday. I'm not sure whether to believe him when he says it's casual. Just because he wears ripped jeans to fancy art openings doesn't mean people won't stare if I do it.

Just then, Petey toddles up to me and smiles. I get low and hold out my hand for a high five. He grasps my finger and scrunches up his face, loudly messing up his diaper. "Jesus, Thatcher." The smell hits the room in a cloud. Petey releases my finger, and he starts to cry. "We have to get him cleaned up," I yell.

"All right. Hm. I don't see the changing pad Alice usually sticks in the bag. Woo, Petey, you outdid yourself." Thatcher rummages through Petey's diaper bag, pulling out tubes of diaper cream and spare clothes. I fan the air, while Petey starts crying louder, so I pick him up, feeling that he's soggy all up his back. I start to bounce him and make shushing sounds.

"What if you put some of that down on the carpet?" I point with my toe at a box of bubble wrap Thatcher has sitting by the door. I guess he uses that to ship his art.

"Great idea! Ok, set him down here."

Together, we strip the soiled clothes off Petey's thrashing body to the chorus of crackles and pops as Petey wriggles around on the bubble wrap. We manage to get the diaper off and we use about 36 wipes scrubbing him from his neck to his knees. He lies on the bubble wrap smiling each time it crackles, while I gather up the messy clothes and the rancid diaper.

"Ok. I'm going to soak these clothes in your utility sink and throw this diaper away outside," I say. "Then I'll come back and it can be your turn to clean up."

"Got it. I'll find Petey some clothes."

I walk through the kitchen of Thatcher's house and open the basement door. I take note that the place is much tidier than I would have thought. Sure, there's wood paneling and 1970s-style wallpaper, but it's neat and it smells clean. The basement isn't even damp. I'm up to my elbows in suds and baby shorts when I hear Thatcher yelling, "No! No! Emma, help! Help!"

I fly up the stairs and into the living room, where Petey is smiling, half dressed, and a shirtless Thatcher Stag is holding an open tube of diaper cream. "Emma! He ate it! I turned away to take off my shirt because it had poop on it and when I looked back at him, he had this in his mouth!"

"Do you remember how full it was before?" I look at the tube. It's organic diaper cream, so I guess there can't be too many harmful ingredients.

Thatcher shakes his head and runs his hands through his hair. He looks panicked. "Go wash your hands, Thatcher. You're getting diaper cream everywhere." I pick up the baby. Thatcher looks down at his fingers and silently walks into the kitchen.

Petey is still laughing and clapping. His face is shiny and his breath smells a little like the cream. I sigh, remembering a story I researched not too long before. I dig out my phone and call up Poison Control.

"Yes, hi. My friend and I are babysitting and the little guy just ate some diaper cream." Thatcher walks back in the room and, seeing me on the phone, starts to panic all over again. I mouth "poison control" to him and he grips my arm while I bounce Petey. "No, I'm not sure--hey Thatcher, how old is Petey and what does he weigh?" He snatches the phone from me and talks with the specialist. Within a few minutes Thatcher collapses to the ground in relief.

"He's going to be fine. Absolutely fine."

Nine

THATCHER

I rest my head against the wall until I feel my heart start to slow down. I seriously thought I had maybe killed my nephew, and now I'm more exhausted than I can ever remember feeling.

Emma, still holding Petey, starts rubbing her nose against his nose. Shit, she was ice cool during all of that. Didn't panic for a minute and she knew exactly what to do. She explained that she had just done a big research project about Poison Control and got to interview some of the people who work in the call center. Even now, she's calm. She says, "Why don't you go take a shower? Petey and I will clean up in here. When you get back I'll finish up down at the utility sink."

I look down at my chest, remembering that I had to take off my stained shirt. I think this might be the only time I've had my shirt off in front of a woman where I wasn't actively trying to take off hers, too. I don't totally get what's going on here, because Emma is seriously sexy, but all I'm feeling right now is gratitude for her. I nod and hurry upstairs. I have to scrub a lot to get all the oily diaper cream off. When I get out of the shower I hear Emma narrating. "We're taking this stinky pile out to the trash. Yes, we are! Yes, that is silly, isn't it? Do you feel better now that you got all that out?"

Fragile Illusion

I walk downstairs and see her holding my nephew, smiling up at me, and I forget for a minute that we are about to start an illusion. This girl is the real deal. Just totally, honestly herself. Wide open. Willing to help me out, even with a baby shit storm. Only now I've roped her into this big lie, and it feels like she's off limits. I plunk a kiss on Petey's head and tell her, "You can go get cleaned up now. I'll try to keep this guy alive while you're down there."

She smiles. I notice that she's totally cleaned up the rug. I didn't even know I had carpet cleaner, but I can tell she scrubbed up some places where the bubble wrap wasn't sufficient barrier. I look at my baby nephew and wonder how such a small person can make such a huge mess. "Petey, man, what the hell did you eat?" He tugs my beard. Seems about right.

Eventually, I hear a car pull up outside. The three of us are sitting on the couch. Emma is coaching Petey through "braiding" my hair. I groan and lean my head on Emma's shoulder. "How the hell am I supposed to tell my brother I almost killed his kid?"

Emma pats my knee. "Petey was never in danger. Poison Control said that brand of cream is as harmless as cream cheese. Just tell Tim what happened."

"You forget that my brother is an asshole." I grit my teeth as the door opens. Alice comes rushing in to take Petey from me and doesn't notice Emma sitting there at first.

"Did you miss Mommy?" She purrs at him, shaking her head and her blonde curls wiggle all around. "Did you have fun here with your uncle and OH MY GOD! Is this her??"

Emma blushes, and Alice shoves Petey into Tim's arms. "I'm Alice Stag." She starts shaking Emma's hand and sits beside her on the couch. She pulls Emma in for a one-armed hug. "We didn't think you were real!! Thatcher, why didn't you say she'd be here tonight? Oh my gosh. You really *do* have a fiancé?"

Emma sort of waves and I clear my throat. "Tim, Alice, this is Emma Cheswick. My beloved." I grin.

Tim makes a sort of grunting sound. He's still pissed off from the other day, but whatever. Alice claps her hands. "Emma! Are you coming to dinner on Sunday? What's your favorite food? I'll make it for you. Did Thatcher tell you I'm a chef? Don't hold back. Tell me your favorite foods."

"Alice, slow your roll," I tell her, but Emma is smiling.

She says, "Thatcher didn't get around to telling me much about his family yet, although I did hear that his brother Tim is a bit of a big deal." Damn, this girl knows how to work a crowd. I wonder if this is how she gets interview subjects to open up to her. Within a few minutes, she's got Alice talking

Fragile Illusion

about her long journey to go to culinary school and how, thanks to Juniper's influence, they now have a daycare right in the office at Stag Law. Petey and their colleague Ben's new son are the only kids in there so far. Alice manages to get Emma to admit Nicky's Thai Kitchen is her absolute favorite place to eat in the city, while they talk about her living on the North Side. Soon, Alice has a whole Thai-themed meal planned out for Sunday and she and Emma look like they've been friends for years.

I sigh, exhaling deeply. I need to tell them about the diaper cream, and I figure it's better now while Alice is over the moon at meeting Emma. "Hey, so, Alice, Petey had quite a diaper incident earlier."

Tim grunts again. "That happens," he says, looking up the leg hole of Petey's new shorts, as if I wouldn't have wiped it all up.

"So anyway," I continue, "It was colossal. Emma had to go soak his clothes in the utility sink, and I looked away for just one second--one fucking second, I swear to you--and Petey ate a bunch of diaper cream." I blow out a breath, anticipating the onslaught.

My brother's face is stony. Irate. "What?"

"Luckily it was the non-toxic kind you had in your diaper bag," Emma pipes in, but Tim interrupts her.

"You need to stay out of this!"

"Tim!!" Alice stands up, looking like she wants to punch my brother.

Tim's face is purple with rage as he looks in Petey's mouth. "Why the fuck are we here and not at children's hospital getting his stomach pumped? Did you even call 911?"

"Hey, woah, Tim. Take it easy, man. I'm trying to tell you. Emma called Poison Control."

"Take it easy? You called some sort of fucking answering service instead of calling medical professionals at--"

"Actually," Emma's own face is set now. Her voice is strong as she starts to correct Tim. "To work at Poison Control, you need to have a PhD in pharmacology or have at least worked in emergency medicine. These are highly skilled medical professionals, far more so than the paramedics who may or may not have only had a short training course, depending what the city has funding for that year."

Tim closes his mouth. He looks at Emma, waits a few beats, like he's trying to process being put in his place along with accepting that his kid is safe. He inhales slowly through his nose and rubs his hands on his temples. "Please tell me what they said at Poison Control."

He directs that question at Emma, and she answers, touching his arm reassuringly. "They said that brand of diaper cream is non-toxic--basically just like cream cheese. For

Peter's age and weight there is absolutely nothing to be worried about."

Tim nods and stoops to pick up the diaper bag. He starts walking out, but Alice says, "Timber Stag. I think you owe Emma an apology." She raises a brow and her violet eyes slice daggers at him. She's clutching Petey to her chest now and he has his head down, like he's about to fall asleep.

Tim sighs. "Emma, I apologize for my tone. I felt frightened for my son's safety and I was out of line to speak to you that way." I marvel at how Alice gets Tim to behave like a human. I've been the target of his snap panic more times than I can count, and I've never gotten an apology when he jumps to conclusions. No wonder he always said Alice drove him crazy when they first met. Marriage really suits him, I guess.

Tim raises his brows and looks back and forth between Emma and Alice. Alice smiles and kisses his cheek, and Emma says, "That's ok. I'd be scared, too, if I'd left my kid with Uncle Thatcher." She winks one of her green eyes and hot damn, if I don't get hard. I cough and adjust my pants, trying not to think about Emma that way.

The mood feels instantly lighter. We walk my family outside and they drive off in their super-safe Volvo. I look around, but I don't see Emma's car.

"Where's your car, Chezz?"

"I don't drive," she says. "I took a Lyft here."

"You don't drive? In Pittsburgh? How the hell does that work?"

She shrugs. "Plenty of people don't have cars. We have buses, you know."

I laugh a bit. "I guess. Well go on and get your stuff. I'll take you home. It's the least I can do for you."

She nods. "Oh I know," she says.

After I drop her off, I notice that my truck smells like her. Like jasmine and mint.

Ten
EMMA

"Cheswick!" Phil has stopped using his admin to summon me, instead just opening his office door to bellow my name across the farm of cubicles. I notice that I'm the only reporter who gets this treatment, and I can't decide if that means he likes me or if my neck is still on the chopping block. "Come on in here."

"Yep," I say, closing the lid to my laptop. I plunk into the seat across from Phil expectantly. I turned in my revised draft of the piece about Thatcher's opening. I stayed up most of the night to work on it, after the diaper incident.

"This is more like it," Phil says, tapping his monitor. "This isn't even a puff piece. You got him to really talk to you."

I smile. Phil never, ever hands out these sorts of compliments. I start to relax a little more, and then Phil says, "I want you to come to the editorial meeting later. Let's hear your ideas for the next few weeks."

My jaw drops. Junior reporters almost never get to go speak up in these meetings. We get whatever assignments nobody else wants. We work the beats, trudge into emergency rooms and interview operators at Poison Control, trying to sniff out our own angle on the assignments. The thought of sharing my idea about Juniper...well, Thatcher's idea...I squeeze my thighs to keep from clapping my hands in excitement.

"That'll be all, Cheswick," Phil says, already typing away on someone else's article submission.

"Thank you, Phil. This means a lot to me."

"Ungh." This time, I can tell his grunt is short for "you're welcome, now beat it and let me work."

I decide to take an early lunch. I text Nicole to see if she can meet me so I can tell her all about it. I practically skip across the bridge to our favorite Thai place--I could eat Thai every day--and I see her already sitting at our table on the back porch.

"Nick! You're not going to believe it!"

"Spill it," she says. She's dressed impeccably, as always, looking like she is off to kill it in the board room. "I've got 46 minutes before I have to pitch our software to an investor."

"Aha, so that's why you're dressed like a superhero today. Anyway!" I start to tell her the extended version of going to Thatcher's house last night, but she cuts me off.

"Wait. You went to that creep's house? Alone? After he practically molested you at the opening? What is wrong with you, Emma?"

"Oh, shit. I forgot I didn't fill you in." I grimace. I'm not supposed to tell anyone about Thatcher's and my plan to fool his family...but this is Nicole. I'm not going to be able to do

Fragile Illusion

this on my own. I need her advice, like always. "So I sort of made a deal with him where I'm pretending to be his fiancé and he's giving me open access to his studio and to his family--which is why I'm excited today and--"

"Hold on." She signals the server to bring her a Thai iced tea. "I need caffeine for this. Start at the beginning and leave nothing out."

Once I explain the whole thing, Nicole has drunk two of those orange iced teas and she's tapping her fingers on the table rapidly, her nails clicking on the Formica. "I think it's weird," she says.

"That's fair," I respond, but explain that it's already paying off in my favor because I get to pitch at the meeting this afternoon. "I didn't even tell Thatcher that I'm going to pitch something his sister-in-law said about daycare in the office. That's, like, a whole third feature I could maybe get in exchange for pretending to like him for a few weeks."

Nicole has her phone out, tapping around, looking for something. "Oh," she says, sliding it across to me. "Is this him? Shit, he's hot."

I look at the picture. It must be an old one, where his beard is shorter and his hair isn't so...ratty. "He does look good there," I say. "He's more hipster, grungy caveman these days, I'd say. Not my type." *Liar,* I think, biting my lip.

"Ha! Girl, you don't have a type."

"I have a not-type," I tell her, diving into the noodles and sliced mango with coconut rice. "I will say, he's really sexy when he's taking care of his nephew, and he has amazing abs."

"Does he know about all your...stuff?" Nicole wipes her mouth and checks her watch. I can tell she's about to scurry off to her meeting.

I shake my head. "I don't see why he needs to know about that," I tell her. "I haven't felt a seizure aura for months. Really, Nick, I'm more worried that he will encounter my mother than I am about him finding out my health quirks." I finger the rose-gold medical alert bracelet that Nicole helped me find when we were in college. *"This one doesn't scream 'there's something wrong with me!'"* she'd said.

When I moved in with her she helped me find a new neurologist, and that was the first time I'd had control over my symptoms. The first time I felt like I could have a life outside of my mother's home, away from her oppressive care. I owe Nicole a lot more than just Pad Thai and friendship. She squeezes my hand. "Kick ass at your meeting, Em."

"You, too, friend." She winks, grabs her purse, and clicks out the door in her heels.

Eleven

THATCHER

My phone buzzes on the metal table across the shop, but I'm holding a steel rod with molten glass on the end, so I can't answer. It buzzes persistently, distracting me from my work. I roll the rod, and the glass gloops off to the side. "Mother fucker!" I yell, tossing it into the bucket of cold water. I can't concentrate today. The phone keeps buzzing.

"What?" I yell into the phone, seeing that it's my brother Tim calling.

"Woah, there, man."

"Tim. I'm working. What's up that you called twice?"

He coughs. "Sorry. Alice asked me to make sure Emma was still coming to family dinner this weekend. She's out buying special lime leaves, apparently."

"Alice has my cell. Why didn't she call herself?" I don't mean to be so snippy with my brother. Actually, maybe I do. He was a dick to me, and he was fucking rude to Emma after that incident with Petey. At least he apologized to *her*.

Tim exhales noisily. I can almost see the veins pulsing in his neck. "She wanted me to call you myself," he says. He doesn't say that Alice has been giving him shit for how he's been treating me and he doesn't apologize, so I keep my cold demeanor.

"Emma and I will be there. I promise." After a beat, I add, "Please thank Alice for buying special food for Emma."

"Will do. See you then." He hangs up.

My concentration is totally wrecked. I can't even remember what I had wanted to do with that piece of glass. I pull the rod from the bucket and tap off the ruined glob. I'm about to dip back into the furnace for more when I hear my phone buzz yet again.

"WHAT?" I roar into the phone without looking at the caller ID.

"Jesus, Stag. I think everyone on the bus just heard you."

"Emma? I'm sorry. I thought you were my brother again. What's up?"

She squeaks. Actually squeaks. I can tell she's excited as she tells me about her meeting with her editor. The guy loved the story she wrote about me after our evening with Petey-- Emma wouldn't let me read it of course. Said I have to wait until it goes to print. But what's really got her excited is that she got to pitch the story about Juniper.

"The whole staff was so pumped about the idea of the feature story about Juniper *and* they love the idea of looking into childcare in the work place. I'm going to do a whole feature, where I look at what Stag Law is doing and talk to some other companies with unique approaches to being family friendly."

I smile, and forget that she can't see me. "That's great, Chezz. I'm really glad this is working out."

"I feel so invigorated!" she says, her voice buzzing. "I can't wait to dive in and write all these stories. SO I wanted to thank you. It's not so bad faking a relationship with you in exchange for this career boost."

"Gee, thanks." I laugh. "Hey, while I have you, my sister in law went and bought special lime juice or something today. She wants to make sure you'll be there Sunday."

"Holy shit! She found kefir lime leaves? Oh my god. This is going to be amazing. I wouldn't miss it."

I make plans to pick her up with enough time to stop at the flower store--she insists she wants to buy a gift for Alice, which is pretty damn cute. I feel really glad that she wants to impress my family. By the time we hang up, I forget that I'm angry and I dive back into my work, ready to create.

Twelve

EMMA

"Oh, god." I wake up Sunday and I just know. I can feel an aura. I haven't been getting enough sleep lately--have been staying up too late doing research. Fuck. If I take my meds, I'll sleep for 12 hours and I absolutely cannot afford to lose an entire day to this, so I take half a dose. I try to go back to bed for just a few hours, but by the time Thatcher is due to pick me up, I'm still nauseated and feeling sluggish.

I can't miss this dinner, not after Alice went out of her way to go and get special ingredients, not when I'm supposed to be doing pre-interviews with Thatcher's relatives. My career depends on this next month. Fuck this *condition*. I close my eyes and press my fingers against my temples, trying to block out the ring of pearlescent light that bathes everything.

I catch a glimpse of the glass sculpture that Thatcher gave me. It reflects the sunlight in my apartment, and for some reason, when I'm staring at it, everything is clear. The light appears normal. *Huh.* Guess I'll just stare at that glass neuron until he gets here. I slip into some passable jeans and grab the nearest clean t-shirt. I decide I have to take Thatcher at his word that dinner will be casual.

I don't hear him knocking. I'm staring at the neurons, trying to hold it together, and suddenly I hear his booming voice. "Emma! Yo! What is going on? Can you let me in? Are you washing your fucking hair or what?"

I exhale deeply and walk to the door, keeping my head as still as possible.

"Oh," he says, seeing me. "You feeling ok?"

I start to shake my head no, which is a mistake, and I have to bite back bile. "Just a touch of a headache," I tell him. "I'll be ok once I eat something."

I hope that's true. I grab my purse and follow Thatcher down the stairs slowly, and I let him help me into the truck. This is why I don't tell people about my condition. I hate the way he's looking at me right now, with pity and like I'm some helpless child. He's not even teasing me or acting rude. I don't want him to act differently just because--oh shit.

"Hey, Stag, please tell me you have pineapple in here and I'm not losing my mind." When I'm about to have a seizure, sometimes I smell things that aren't really there. Thatcher's whole truck smells like tropical fruit right now.

He lifts a plastic bag from the floor near my feet. "I brought fruit. I knew Alice was doing Thai so I grabbed pineapple and mango from Whole Paycheck earlier. You've got a good nose."

Relief floods through me. If I'm not smelling things that aren't there, I might be ok. I might make it through without humiliating myself and ruining his family dinner. I lean my head back on the headrest just as Thatcher puts an arm around the back of my seat. I look over at him as he turns to look behind him to back out of the parking spot. *Shit, that's hot.* He's got one hand on the wheel and his grey eyes are tight with concentration. The way my aura is working right now, his head is sort of glowing. I notice how attractive he is, under all that hair and beard. I can see the strong bones of his face, the tight muscles in his shoulders and forearms.

He catches me staring and grins. "Are you undressing me with your eyes, Chezz?" He shifts the truck into gear and heads toward the highway.

"Don't flatter yourself." I close my eyes and say, "don't forget I want to stop and grab some flowers for Alice."

"Check the bag, Chezz," he says, merging onto Route 28. "I clipped some lilac from out back. Alice loves lilacs." Sure enough, he's got a mason jar with fat, white blooms, tied in twine. His thoughtfulness surprises me. He really knows his family well, cares about them. *Why does he need a fake fiancé?* I decide to press him about it later. For now, I need to close my eyes and pray I can keep my wits about me.

By the time we get to the Stag homestead, as I've been imagining it, the place is brimming with people. Thatcher leads me around to the back yard, where clusters of picnic tables and coolers dot the yard. I see kids blowing bubbles while adults stand chatting, animatedly. Everyone looks so comfortable, so happy to be there. My family "picnics" are loosely veiled political fundraisers where everyone wears suits and stands stiffly, drinking from real glasses.

This just feels like comfort. I even feel my aura ease up in the shaded yard that smells of honeysuckle and cooking food. This could be ok. Alice pops out of the back door carrying a tray of skewered meat and vegetables. When she sees Thatcher and me, she shoves the tray into someone's hands and comes running through the yard. "You made it! I'm so glad!"

She pulls me in for a hug and I have to quickly move the flowers out of the way. I flush, feeling badly at taking advantage of her kindness with our illusion, but I hand her the blooms. She buries her nose into the flowers and says, "I love them. I'm going to put them on the windowsill." She links her arm through mine. "Come with me into the kitchen and meet Juniper."

Alice passes me around to all the women inside the house--her sister, Amy, who is hugely pregnant with her third son but still making it through three 12-hour nursing shifts each week; Anna Stag, the brothers' grandmother who lives on the third floor of Tim and Alice's house; and Juniper Jones. The bride to be, focus of my next feature assignment. Her smile is warm as she greets me. "Thatcher hasn't told us a thing about you," she says, "So we're all dying to know everything."

Lainey Davis

63

"Everything," says Anna, shoving a drink toward me. "Drink up and spill, Emma."

"Oh," I say. "I don't drink alcohol, actually. Is there maybe some water?"

Amy raises an eyebrow at me and pats her stomach. "Any particular reason you're off the booze? Is this why Thatcher is suddenly engaged out of the blue?"

Alice claps her hands and Juniper's jaw drops. Their grandmother laughs and slaps the counter. They all stare at me. I flush, my body filled with heat. "No! Oh my god. No. I just...I can't...there's a medication I take and I..."

My voice trails off. I don't want to explain all of this. Anna actually looks disappointed, and starts chugging the drink she'd prepared for me. Thankfully, Amy walks over with another glass. "Try this," she says. "It's watermelon blended with coconut milk and mint. You *almost* won't miss the rum that's not in it."

I exhale and take a sip. It's delicious--refreshing enough that my nausea passes and the weird glow of my aura subsides a little further. I thank her and brace myself for the inquisition that follows. By the time Alice is ready to announce dinner, I've given them the full lie Thatcher and I had planned out about how we met, reinforced that we don't want to steal from Juniper and Ty's celebration by making a big deal of our engagement, and I even managed to get

Juniper's work number to call her this week about an interview.

"My coach will be beside himself about the publicity," she says. Everything is going so well. I sit down by Thatcher, who drapes an arm over my shoulder and glares at me when I instinctively stiffen. I try to relax, and then I sink my teeth into Alice's Thai feast and I feel like I could stay here forever, eating myself into oblivion.

Thirteen
THATCHER

"Emma seems cool, bro," Ty whispers as she walks over to get more food. "She's real down to earth compared to...well. She's cool." Ty sighs. I know he's remembering some of the other women I've brought to his games. Flashy women who never dress appropriately for an ice rink, but who never mind because I'm always happy to whisk them away and warm them up.

Ty's right about Emma. She's nothing like any of those women. She's totally at home here in jeans and a well-loved t-shirt with a pair of Toms. And she's eating, right in front of my family. As a matter of fact, I feel like I need to lean over and protect my bowl of Tom Kha soup so Emma doesn't steal it from me. I see why she got so excited to learn Alice had driven all over the place for the ingredients. I need to make more requests from Alice, because this shit is delicious. I slurp the last of the broth and swallow, clapping Ty on the back. "Thanks, Ty. She's all right I guess."

He laughs at what he thinks is just a wry joke. "How come she doesn't have an engagement ring?"

Shit. He noticed. "Well..." I need to stall. Emma and I hadn't really talked about this, but she comes to my rescue.

"I don't need one. I told Thatcher I'd rather we spend the money on a down payment for a house." I could kiss her for thinking so fast, but I promised I'd be a gentleman, so I settle for stroking her cheek. I only touch her because my family has to buy that we're a couple in love, so I'm a little taken aback by the spark of heat I feel when I connect with her skin. Maybe she's just hot. She looks a little pale, come to think of it, but she smiles for an instant before her face drops back to a worried look. She seems off, but I can only concentrate on her scent as she leans against my arm. She smells nice, fruity and fresh but not overpowering. *Different from the last time,* I think, then feel unsettled that I'm remembering her different scents. This is unexpected.

The conversation around the table shifts and everyone starts helping with cleanup. I notice Emma seems to be struggling a little to stand up. "Hey," I whisper into her ear. "You ok?"

She nods slightly, but doesn't meet my eyes. "Just...maybe I need some water."

"Stay here. I'll grab some for you." I walk over to the cooler to grab a bottle of water but I hear someone scream.

"Thatcher!"

I look up and Emma is on the ground. Her body is stiff and Amy is crouched over her. I can't tell what's going on, so I rush over, then I see her face and I freeze in shock and fear.

"Thatcher," Amy's voice comes through my fog and I look at her, still not speaking. "What do we need to know about Emma? She said she takes medication?"

"I...I..." I struggle for words. I have no fucking clue what Amy is talking about. I barely know this girl and she's having some sort of convulsions on the lawn of my brother's house. Emma's face is stiff, her eyes unseeing. Her body twitches violently on the lawn. A minute passes and she turns her head sharply and vomits in the grass.

I notice Amy fumbling around with Emma's arm, tugging on the bracelet she always wears. I squint and notice that the rose-colored metal has one of those snake symbols on it. A Medic Alert bracelet. *Huh.* "Ok we need to get her to the emergency department," Amy says. "Emma has epilepsy, but I don't know if she's had her rescue medications or how long she's been seizing."

I can't seem to move or concentrate. "Seizing?" None of this makes sense. Wouldn't I have been able to tell if she had epilepsy?

"Thatcher!" Alice's sister is yelling at me and shaking my shoulders. "Pick her up and carry her to the car. We're going to the hospital." I do as she says and climb in the back seat of Amy's minivan with Emma. I have no idea what to do.

Amy climbs in the drivers seat and Alice leans in the window to hand me a package of wet wipes. "So you can clean

Fragile Illusion

her up a little bit," Alice says, patting my hand. I look at Emma and nod. Her body is relaxed now, but she's totally zonked.

"Amy, what the hell is going on here?"

Amy looks at me in the rear view mirror. "Hasn't this happened before? How long have you been together?"

I try to dodge that question. "Never, Aim. I have never seen her like this."

Amy sighs. "Some people go months without a big seizure, especially if they're managing their medications. From what Emma said in the kitchen she must be pretty careful."

"She did say she wasn't feeling awesome, but I didn't know that meant...what should I do?"

I see Amy shrug as she pulls into the turn-around at the hospital. "At this point we probably just give her some benzos and let her sleep. But they'll probably have her info on file." Amy parks the van. "Carry her inside and I'll meet you in there after I park. Tell whoever's in triage that you're with me."

I carry Emma's sleeping form inside and drop Amy's name. They take me right back to a small room with a gurney, so I get Emma situated. Her clothes are a wreck. The nurse asks if I want help getting Emma into a gown, and it feels wrong for me to undress her in this state, so I nod and step back while she works. I turn away and see Amy bustling down the hallways as fast as a hugely pregnant person can shuffle.

She gives me the side eye and helps the nurse lift Emma's hips to take off her jeans. I feel myself flush at the sight of Emma's pink flowered panties, and I turn away, feeling super uncomfortable about this whole situation.

I hear a young, deep voice finishing a phone call and look up to see a man in scrubs, carrying an iPad. "Amy, didn't think I'd see you until Tuesday. What've we got here?"

"Oh, Jeremy. I'm glad it's you. Listen, this is my brother-in-law's fiancé. Wait. Are you my brother in law? This is my sister's brother in law...his brother is married to--"

"Amy, spare me the ancestry report. What's wrong?"

"Emma had a seizure. Her medic alert bracelet says she has epilepsy but I don't know what meds she takes, if she took her rescues, anything. Thatcher here has just been totally numb with worry, which is sweet, but useless."

I don't even bother to scowl at her, because I do feel sort of shell-shocked. I pretend I'm too upset to remember her birth date, but I manage to spell Emma's last name for the doctor, who clicks around in his iPad. "Cheswick, Cheswick...here we go. Hm." He looks down at Emma and starts to examine her. I hear him ask the nurse for something that sounds like ox, which can't be right, but he lifts one of her eyelids and shines a light in her eye. They hook some machines up to Emma while I shift my weight uncomfortably.

"Listen," Dr. Jeremy says to me. "You're not listed on her chart, so I need to call what I assume are her parents. I can't say much more than that, even to a colleague who isn't on duty." I nod and he gives some info to another person in scrubs. I look over at Amy with a pained expression.

Amy scowls and says, "Hypothetically, Jeremy, if a patient presented unconscious after a tonic-clonic seizure, what would your treatment be?"

Jeremy smiles and squeezes my arm. "Hypothetically, I'd check out her heart rate and her oxygen levels, do some tests, but mostly give her some meds to help her sleep and discharge her after she woke up. I'd have this hypothetical patient follow up with her neurologist on Monday...except I believe I saw this patient's hypothetical neurologist in the coffee shop a few minutes ago. If you'll excuse me, I feel the need for caffeine."

Amy smiles as he walks down the hallway.

"What the hell just happened here?" I ask her. I really feel like my head is spinning.

"She's going to be fine. They called her parents to fill them in, so you'll probably see them soon. Are they as nice as Emma?"

Oh shit, I think. Suddenly our innocuous plan is dragging us both deeper into the damn swamp. Why does everything have to be so fucking complicated?

Fourteen
EMMA

When I wake up, I have no idea where I am, but I know I've had a seizure. *Shit.* It's been months. Months! My head aches, but the aura is gone and I feel, above all, complete relief. My senses and awareness slowly catch up to me, and I hear a familiar, unwelcome voice.

"I just don't understand what's going on here at all. Edward, *who* are these people? Who is this *caveman* in Emma's room? Why is she still down here and not in a private room upstairs? Where is that doctor? Edward?" My mother is on one of her rants, and I start putting things together before I attempt to open my eyes.

I must be in the hospital, which means they called my damn parents. I remember feeling better, but then worse and asking Thatcher to get me some water after dinner. The rest is totally gone. *Caveman...*

I open my eyes and I see Thatcher sitting in a chair across the room. He looks worried. His legs are spread wide and he's hunched over on his elbows, his chin in his hands. Amy is here, too. She struggles to stand up and I hear her friendly voice talking to my mother. "You must be Mrs. Cheswick! I'm so glad to meet you. I'm Amy. Alice's sister."

My father scowls, adjusting his tie. "And just who is Alice?" His voice is toneless. I can see him classifying Thatcher and Amy as unimportant.

"Thatcher," Amy looks at him uncomfortably. "Introduce me to Emma's parents."

"I can assure you," my mom cuts in, "that I have never seen this man before in my life."

Amy opens her mouth to start saying something, and I decide now is a good time for a distraction. I groan and try to sit up.

"Oh, dear. You're awake." My mother bustles over to the bed and puts the back of her hand against my forehead. "I just knew this was bound to happen."

"Of course, Mom. I have seizures because I have epilepsy. Not because I moved into the city."

She clucks her tongue at me and starts asking a million questions about "this new aged neurologist" she doesn't approve of. Just because the guy she and dad sent me to for years couldn't control my symptoms and would never try any new medications...or even read about trials that might be helpful. "This is a research hospital, Mom. They know what they're doing here."

My father snorts and my mother looks over at Thatcher and Amy again. "Emma, shouldn't your *friends* be heading home now, dear?" I hate her tone. I hate everything about the

Fragile Illusion

way my parents judge anyone who doesn't seem like they're going to cut a huge campaign donation.

"Look," Amy's on her feet now, and a pregnant, frustrated Amy is apparently no one to be trifled with. "I don't know why you'd talk about Emma's fiancé this way, but I'm going to assume you're all just upset and in shock. So I'm going to go home and eat dessert. Thatcher, call me later."

Amy saunters out of the room just as the word "fiancé" registers with my mother.

"Fiancé?" she repeats it about six times, her voice increasing an octave each time. "Don't be *ridiculous,* Emma. You cannot marry someone like...you cannot marry this man. Do you even know this man? Where did you meet?"

"Look, Mrs. Cheswick," now Thatcher is on his feet. "You really don't get to talk about me this way. I don't give a shit who you are or how much your pearls cost. I'm here to support Emma and my guess is she has a pretty bad headache right now, so you're going to need to tone it down or I'm going to get someone to escort you out."

My face breaks into the biggest smile I can remember smiling. Nobody ever speaks to my mother this way. I want to watch as she sputters and tries to gather her wits, but even being awake this long has been difficult. My body needs to sleep.

Lainey Davis

"Emma Cheswick," she hisses at me. "Are you engaged to be *married* to this barbarian?"

"Mom, Dad, this is Thatcher Stag," I croak. "And he's right about the headache. I promise to tell you all about him when I wake up, but for now I need to go back to sleep." I feel the medication kicking in. They must have given me an IV. Yes, there. I can feel it in my hand now that I focus on it. I am vaguely aware of my mother and father arguing, then leaving the room. I drift off, sinking into sleep.

I wake up again. I know I'm in the hospital, but I have no idea how much time has passed. I don't hear anyone in my room. I feel the urge to stretch, and find that I can, easily, though my muscles are aching. When I try to sit up, I see that Thatcher is still in my room. That's unexpected.

"Hey," he says. "You're up." He puts down a notebook where he'd been writing something. Sketching?

"What time is it?" There are no windows in my room. Am I still in the emergency department?

"Well, Chezz," he says, reaching for a cup of coffee. "It's about 9am."

I sit bolt upright. "It's Monday? Shit!" I start to get out of the bed, flinging the IV line, but Thatcher walks over and touches my arm.

"Hey," he says. "Don't be mad at me. But I called the receptionist at the Post and told her you were sick. I didn't say with what."

"You did that for me?" I look into his eyes. "That was very thoughtful, Thatcher. Thank you." I am definitely in no shape to go to work today. But I still feel desperate to get home. I hate that I've lost most of a day. I'm going to be so behind on work and--then I remember. I had a seizure at Thatcher's family dinner. "Your family. What must they think of me?" I bury my hands in my hair, tugging in frustration.

"Well, they've called here about 8 million times, worried sick and asking why I didn't tell them you have epilepsy."

I snort. "Because it's none of their damn business."

"Well I guess that's why you didn't tell *me* you have epilepsy, then." Thatcher scratches his beard. "So what does all this mean?" He gestures around the room.

I sigh. "It means I felt this coming on yesterday, but I didn't want to cancel on you...or Alice, so I didn't take the medication I should have. It was stupid. I haven't had a seizure in--well, it's been over a year."

"Emma, you don't have to put your health at risk for this...me. I--"

"This is why I don't tell people, Stag." I snap at him. "I don't want your pity or your deep concern or your fake, polite kindness. We both know that's not you. I don't tell people

Lainey Davis

because I don't want to be treated differently or given a pass for family dinner. It's my business. I'm an adult."

"Ok, ok. Chill out, Chezz. Jesus."

"Oh, so I'm 'Chezz' now and not 'sweetheart?'"

Thatcher gives me an odd look and throws a plastic bag at me. "I got your keys from your purse and got you some fresh clothes from your apartment."

I look down at the bag. This is so totally unexpected that I have no idea how to respond. This is something Nicole would do. This is a friend move. I don't trust many people to know what I need without my having to ask them for help. I swallow.

He chugs the rest of his coffee and throws the cup in the trash. "Why don't you get dressed and I'll drive you home. Your doctor said you were good to go whenever you woke up." I nod slowly and he steps into the hall, pulling the curtain closed around the doorway as he leaves the room.

Fragile Illusion

Fifteen
THATCHER

I start pacing the halls of the emergency department, waiting for Emma to get dressed. This whole thing is getting really intense. After she fell asleep and her parents left, I drove around the city for a long time, just trying to calm down. No wonder she's secretive and private, if her parents are like that. I know I don't look like my brother Tim, between all my piercings and tattoos and facial hair. But who the fuck wants to look like that? Fuck Emma's dad for thinking that's the only way to hold value in the world.

I've got a piece of my glass in the damn MOMA for fuck's sake. I'm not sure why I care so much what this guy thinks of me. I see assholes like him all the time. Emma and I have 3 weeks of this left and then we're going to part ways. She and I are about as different as two people can be. I don't see us hanging out socially after this whole thing is said and done.

I'm about to turn around and walk back to her room, make sure she's safe to walk to the car, when I see something that makes my blood run cold. I feel my throat closing, my heart racing, the muscles in my limbs spasming as I clutch the wall.

My father is lying on one of the beds in the ER.

I stand opposite his room, staring at his form on the bed. I know it's him, even though I haven't laid eyes on him for over a decade. He sank into a depression and buried himself in a bottle when our mom died, leaving us home with only Tim to parent us. But you don't forget what your dad looks like. Momentarily breaking my trance, I huff out a laugh, noticing my father and I have the same hairdo and facial hair these days. I hope my fucking beard doesn't look like his, though. Christ, I can smell the urine on him from across the hall.

I'm clutching the wall, breathing heavy, staring at him, when a nurse comes walking down the hall. "Oh," she says. "Hello! Are you here to take Ted home?"

"Excuse me?" My eyes go wide. Take him home?

"You must be related to him," she says. "You look exactly like him." She sighs. "He's what we call a frequent flyer. We never see any family in here with him."

That shakes me back to consciousness. "Yeah, because he fucking walked out on his family and drank away our livelihood." I punch the wall, not caring that I'll have bruised knuckles and won't be able to shape glass today. Fuck. I haven't let myself feel angry at him for a long time.

"I'm sorry, sir." The nurse grits her teeth. She must see a lot of angry family members here in this department.

"I'm sorry...Robin, is it? You don't need to be hearing that from me."

She nods and makes her way down the hall. Lord. What am I supposed to do now? I can't just fucking walk out of here now that I know my fucking father is lying across the hall from Emma.

"FUCK!" I let myself scream just once. Hardly anyone is around at this time of day. Nobody even looks at me, except him.

He opens his eyes and turns his head my way, and our eyes lock. I stand, breathing through my nose, staring at the man who walked out on our family, who forced Tim into a role he shouldn't have had to worry about until his own son was born. I've thought about this moment, about what I would do if I ever saw my father again. In some versions of my fantasy, I beat the shit out of him. Sometimes I cuss him out, screaming in his face until my veins throb and my voice is raw. Most often, I make eye contact and then walk away.

Today, faced with the reality of seeing him, I stand frozen and silent. Staring.

"Son." His voice is hoarse, wavering. It snaps me back into full consciousness.

"It's Thatcher," I spit at him, still shouting from across the hallway.

His eyes flare for a moment. "You think I don't know which one you are?"

"I think you don't think about us at all," I shout back at him, and a passing employee shoots daggers at me with her eyes. I step closer to my father's room, hovering in the doorway. "I think you lost the right to speak to me casually when you walked the fuck out of our lives."

He closes his eyes. "I know I don't deserve your kindness right now."

"You're fucking right you don't." I make to walk back toward Emma's room, but his next words freeze me in my tracks again.

"I'm dying, son."

As I stand there breathing deeply, the thin metal frame of the dividing wall supporting my full weight, Emma emerges from down the hall. She gives me a watery smile and makes her way toward me, tentatively. "Sorry about earlier," she says. "Who's this?"

I don't look at him. I take Emma's elbow and guide her toward the exit. "Nobody," I tell her. "Let me take you home."

Sixteen
EMMA

Thatcher tries to lift me into his truck and I swat away his arm. "I can get in the damn truck by myself," I growl at him. But it's hard to climb up into the cab with my muscles aching. I'm exhausted, and realizing I need his help after all just pisses me off worse. My body feels like I got hit by this truck rather than lifted into it. "This is why I don't tell anyone," I say, resting my head against the glass. "Now you think of me as some victim."

I expect Thatcher to come back at me, for us to argue and fight about how he does or does not treat me, but he just stares ahead as he crosses the bridge to take me to my apartment. I close my eyes eventually, resting for the short trip, until he parks outside my door. I climb out of the truck and turn to thank him for giving me a ride, but he's already gotten out of the truck. He surprises me by following me up the steps and inside my duplex.

"I can...uh...take it from here, I'm pretty sure."

He sighs. "Cheswick, can I come in?"

I wrinkle my brow at him. "I guess so? You know I'm just going to go to bed, right?"

He nods and follows me up. I toss my stuff on the counter and stare at him. He leans against a column with his hands in his jeans pocket. "The guy at the hospital? That was my father."

"Your dad?"

He shakes his head adamantly. "Tim is my 'dad.' That guy was my biological father, who walked out on us, left us all for a bottle of booze when my mom died and he couldn't handle...all of it."

"What's wrong with him? Shouldn't you go back to the hospital and sit with him instead of me?"

Thatcher sinks into the couch and I join him, looking at him expectantly. He leans his head back against the wall with enough force that it rattles the pictures I have hung there. "He just told me he's dying. I haven't seen him in over ten years."

I don't really know what to say to this revelation from him, so I slide closer and grab his hand, giving him a squeeze. His skin is warm and smoother than I expected from someone who works with his hands all day. "Tell me more," I say.

Thatcher begins to talk, telling me about the car accident that killed his mother, how their grandmother moved in afterward to help with the needs of 3 young, motherless boys, and how Ted Stag drank more and more, helped less and less, until he lost his job. The boys were a handful, and Anna Stag wasn't always up to the work of parenting 3 angry Stags. Eventually Ted drifted away from their house, not to be heard from again. The Stag brothers lived on a life insurance payout and social security checks that Tim apparently had to cash using slightly-nefarious deception so nobody official became aware that the boys technically had no legal guardian at home.

"That's a really heavy burden your brother took on," I say. I hear echoes of my father's voice booming through my head about "lazy" people who "game the system" to receive handouts, who abuse safety net services. Then I remember what my mother said about Thatcher in the hospital.

"Holy shit, Thatcher. I'm sorry to interrupt you. I just need to apologize for what my mother said to you. My god, that was inexcusable." I pull his hand to my chest, pleading with him. I'm overcome with embarrassment. He's pouring his heart out to me, took care of me after I had a seizure at his family dinner party, and my mother called him a caveman.

He laughs, a bitter sound. "She's not wrong, is she? I'm the son of a deadbeat, I'm covered in ink, and I'm having inappropriate thoughts about her daughter."

I flush at this last bit, but choose to ignore it. "Thatcher, I can't tell you how sorry I am that you were put in a position where you had to endure someone speaking to you that way. I try and I try to distance myself from my parents, but sometimes..."

"They always come back to fuck with us, don't they?" He reaches out and tucks my hair behind my ear. The gesture surprises me as much as his words of understanding.

Lainey Davis

"Yes," I whisper. And then I just stare at him for a long time. We sit in quiet together, just feeling each other's heartache. Finally I can't stay awake any longer and I tell him, "I really need to go to bed now."

"I'll be here when you wake up," he says.

"Don't be ridiculous," I start to argue with him. He touches a finger to my lips to shush me. I bite my lip and my eyes go wide.

"My family has been blowing up my phone for hours," he reminds me. "They're never going to buy it if I don't stay here and take care of you. Alice is going to drop off some food later, in fact, after she serves lunch at Stag Law. Go on and sleep. Wait. Tell me your Wi-Fi password, and then go sleep."

Seventeen
THATCHER

While Emma sleeps, I pace her living room. I try to sketch out some ideas in my notebook, but I keep thinking back to my father in that bed. Dying, he said. How many times had I prayed for him to just go on and die? To be finally and definitely gone from our lives versus *choosing* to leave us for some other sort of life?

I'm itching to get back in my studio, but my family would give me endless shit if I left Emma here after having a seizure. When Alice texts me that she's outside with some food, I leap up and open the door so quickly, it startles her.

"Hey, sorry about that." I pull the takeout containers from her before she drops them. "Want to come in?" Should I be inviting Alice into Emma's house? I don't really know the etiquette for fake-fiancé personal space.

"Just for a minute," Alice says. "I want to write down info about the food for Emma."

Alice pulls out a notepad and starts taking notes on each container. She seems to have brought an entire week's worth of meals, all sorted and arranged. "Jesus, Alice. This is so much food!"

Alice nods. "Don't you eat a bite of it, either. It's not for you. Hands off." Alice has baggies of herbs and toppings for tacos, fresh bread to go with soup, chicken parm with sauce in a separate container and..."Alice! Did you make pasta from scratch today?"

"Yes. I'm writing Emma a note that she should probably eat the noodles first. They'll be really good today. Let me tell you, Juniper really enjoyed those at lunch! The Stag Law staff all ate very well today." Alice finishes her manual of notes and sighs, smiling.

"Ok, I have to get back to the office. I want to give Petey a squeeze, but I wanted to talk with you about this weekend."

"This weekend?"

Alice rolls her eyes at me. "Do you ever open your computer? There was a whole email chain."

"Who was on the chain?"

Alice bites her lip. "Well, it was mostly me and Juniper and Ty. But you and Tim were included, I swear! And if you give me Emma's email I can loop her in."

"Loop her into what, Alice?"

"Ty and Juniper wanted a Stag Weekend. Instead of a bachelor party or bachelorette party? Get it--Stag? Thatcher, I absolutely know you were with us when we started planning...anyway! Obviously Emma is invited, but I wanted to find out from you if she would be feeling up to going."

I'm about to tell Alice Emma will, in fact, not feel up to a weekend away with the Stag clan, which means I should probably stay home with her to help her "recuperate," when a woman with voluminous blond waves, stiletto heels, and an impeccable manicure opens the door to Emma's apartment.

"Well, well, well," she says, looking at me. "So it is true." The woman tosses a cardigan over one of the stools at Emma's counter and then stands in a model pose in the middle of the room, crossing her arms and glaring at me. Alice looks back and forth between us, speechless for the first time since I met her.

"Can I help you?" I have to tread lightly here, because I have no idea who this woman is but can't let Alice know that Emma and I are basically strangers.

"When Mom called me hysterical crying because Emma is apparently engaged to a 'street fighter,' I had to come see for myself what all the commotion was. I am going to murder her just as soon as she gets her ass out here. She *knew* I was planning to announce my engagement to Logan this weekend! She just had to steal my thunder. As per usual."

Alice raises an eyebrow and opens her mouth to speak. I can tell she's about to launch into defense mode, so I place my hand on her shoulder. "Hey, Al, why don't you go back to work and hug your baby and let me handle this, ok? I'll call you when Emma wakes up and we will talk about the weekend." I usher Alice out the door. I'm pretty used to this sort of treatment from "upstanding" citizens. Sure, they all want a piece of my rogue artwork for their great room, because some critic called my glass "haunting and de rigueur." But none of them want to mingle with me outside of a gallery space. Which is fine with me, because these people drive me crazy.

I close the door behind my sister-in-law and stand opposite the intruder. "I assume you're the perfect sister?"

She snorts and flings her hair back over one shoulder. "I'm Veronica Cheswick, yes. And don't think I didn't Google you. I know you were seen last week, leaving a club with a woman who was not my sister, so don't feed me some bullshit line about being desperately in love with Emma. What's your game, Stag? Why is she set on spoiling my engagement announcement?"

I am taken aback to realize other people look at pictures of me online, leaving clubs with the women I fuck. What the hell else is out there about me in cyberspace? Alice is right--I need to open my computer more often. I pull it together, though, and retort to Veronica. "I can assure you Emma had no intention of spoiling your engagement announcement. She and I have kept our relationship on the D-L because, as I'm sure you saw during your research, my own brother is getting married and neither of us wanted to take away from his moment."

I can tell Veronica doesn't buy it entirely, but she starts tapping her foot and looks around. "Where is my sister, anyway?"

"She's in bed," I say, and then, feeling bold, I add, "where the hell does she usually go after a seizure?"

Veronica sighs, and a look of concern crosses her face. "She hasn't had a big one for awhile," she says, her voice quiet. "Mom is hysterical, and deflecting by freaking out about how it will look if Emma marries someone with tattoos and facial piercings."

"What the hell does anyone care how it looks if Emma's happy?"

This pulls a laugh from Veronica. "Oh, my. Thatcher Stag, you have a lot to learn about the Cheswick family." She picks up her sweater. "Tell Emma I stopped by and please have her call me when she's out of her fog." Veronica heads back out the door. At the last minute, she turns around and says, "She gets really, really sore after a big seizure. I brought her some Tiger Balm." She hands me the tiny tin of ointment and clacks out of Emma's apartment.

When Veronica leaves, I exhale deeply and sink into the couch. This tiny lie to get my brother off my back is becoming a huge, heavy web of confusion. I just want to get back to my life where I spend my afternoons creating amazing fucking artwork, my nights partying hard, and my mornings sleeping it all off. I am grateful to Veronica for at least distracting me from my father for a few minutes.

Thinking on what she said as she left, I text Juniper to ask if she knows any massage therapists who make house calls. I figure if I'm about to spring a weekend out of town with my family on Emma, the least I can do is butter her up first. I set up an appointment for tomorrow afternoon and then I decide it's been too long since I slept. I kick back onto Emma's couch and fall asleep in seconds.

Eighteen
EMMA

I feel so much better when I wake up. My muscles ache, my neck throbs in particular, but my head is clear. My relief is overwhelming, almost like I needed to have that seizure to feel normal again. I hadn't even realized I felt it building. I stretch and look at the clock. Five pm. I have basically been asleep for an entire day since having the seizure, which means my inbox will be full and I'll have about ten messages from my mother in my voicemail. I decide to shower, find food, and then tackle my phone.

After marinating in the hot water for much longer than usual, I wrap a towel around my head and walk into the kitchen. One of my favorite perks of living alone, I decide, is the ability to sit stark naked at my counter and eat without worrying about getting food on my shirt.

I whistle, marveling at how clear my head feels, and walk to the sink to fill the coffee pot. While I turn on the water, I happen to look toward the living room and I scream.

I drop the pot to the tile floor, and the glass shatters as I keep screaming.

Thatcher Stag sits up on my couch, rubbing the sleep from his eyes and then staring at me, open-mouthed. "Shit," he says.

"What the fuck are you doing here?" My voice is shrill and, having nothing in my hands, I move to cover my breasts and crotch.

"Don't move," he says, walking toward me.

"Don't come near me!! I'm naked."

He keeps approaching. "I can see that, Emma, and I'll try to look away, ok, but there's broken glass and you're barefoot."

I start looking around, wildly, unsure how to proceed here. Thatcher steps into his sneakers and walks toward me. "Woah," he says. "You have red pubes."

"Fuck you, Thatcher!" This is like a nightmare.

"I'm sorry, I'm sorry," he says, walking toward me and averting his eyes. "I just...the women I sleep with don't really ever have pubic hair. So..."

"Can you spare me the sexy storytime?"

He nods, keeping his head turned. As he approaches me in the kitchen, he reaches toward my head. I stiffen, but he's pulling the towel off my hair. "Here," he says, his voice surprisingly gentle. "You can cover up with this." He walks toward the fridge, where I have the dustpan and broom wedged between the appliance and the wall, and I hastily wrap the towel around my body. I stand stock still as he stoops to clean up the glass.

"What are you still doing here?" I whisper.

He pours the fragments into the trash and squints, looking around the kitchen. "I think I got it all," he says, "but just to be safe." He picks me up effortlessly and carries me over to the hall, placing me down as I stare at him with wide eyes. "I told you I'd be here when you woke up," he says, shrugging. "Go on and get dressed. I have to tell you what happened."

Five minutes later, when I'm safely dressed in sweats, Thatcher reminds me that my parents were rude, tells me how my sister stopped by to complain and maybe gloat, and he shows me the feast Alice left. Since there's no way I can eat all this before it goes bad, and since I've just about gotten over my humiliation at Thatcher seeing me naked, I decide to share the chicken parm and fresh pasta with him. He did, after all, hang out while I slept to make sure I was ok. Twice.

He makes me laugh, impersonating my sister's hair toss while we wait for the water to boil for the noodles Alice hand rolled this morning. I fill him in on my family, avoiding eye contact. "My dad is a state senator," I tell him. "Our politics are polar opposites, Thatcher. I disagree with almost every measure he supports."

Thatcher tests a noodle and moans. "These are done," he says, shutting off the burner and draining the pasta. "Look, Emma. You can't help who your parents are and neither can I. Don't feel bad about that shit."

"Yeah, but it's not so easy figuring out how to navigate *seeing* your parents whose choices you hate, is it?" I know I've got him there. He's clearly thinking about seeing his father in the hospital as we go on to eat in silence. As soon as Thatcher finishes, he rinses his dishes and stands beside me.

"Don't make any plans after work tomorrow," he tells me. "I have a surprise for you." I raise an eyebrow, but he won't elaborate. "Call me when you get home from work, ok? We need to talk." He sidles out of the apartment, and I try not to stare at his ass as he leaves. Or the way his shoulder muscles move inside his t-shirt. *Shit,* I think. *He just saw me naked.* Thatcher Stag has probably seen a thousand women naked, and he basically admitted he was only taking a clinical interest in my bush. *Of course* the supermodels he fucks don't have pubic hair. There's no reason to think that he might still be thinking of this as anything but a mutually beneficial, non-sexual arrangement. I remind myself that he also saw me seizing on the ground at his brother's house, throwing up...but he didn't run away screaming.

Rather than think about why it would bother me so much if he had, I decide to read my emails and check my voicemails. After I call Nicole.

"Talk to me, Emma. You've been radio silent since the Reindeer party." I hit the major points of the disaster that was the past 24 hours while she runs on the treadmill in her office. "Do you need me to come over with tequila?" she asks.

"I know you're joking," I tell her. "But I appreciate the sentiment."

Nineteen
THATCHER

I can't get the image of Emma out of my head. She stood naked and gleaming in the sunlight in her kitchen. And even though her face was contorted in shock at me seeing her naked, I still have this memory of her bathed in light, glowing. She looked ephemeral. Supernatural. And so fucking perfect. Her body is everything, all curves and soft lines. Creamy skin. And Christ. That hair. Her red hair. Knowing I can't haul her into her bedroom and ravage her body, I settle for the next best thing to unleash all this energy. I drive as fast as I can and rush into my studio to work some glass.

I dip into the furnace and gather a ball of molten glass and sit to shape it at my work bench. Pulling long fragments, twisting, sprinkling on color, I work in a frenzy. I know hours pass. I sense the light shifting in the studio as the sun sets, but I don't want to stop even to turn on the overhead lights. I work by the light of the furnace as I sculpt the tendrils of glass just so, angle the reds and golden threads until I'm satisfied. This work is my lust, my anger, my fear. This is Emma, contorted with illness and rising in triumph. This piece is everything, passion and depth. So much color.

I haven't felt that inspired in months. I exhale and sit back, staring at what I've made. This is light and fury and fire. I

98   *Fragile Illusion*

shape a base so it will rest, stable, and then slide it into the kiln to slowly come down to room temperature, so the fragile material won't shatter.

Only then do I pause and breathe. I just sit in stillness. I feel so fucking calm after I've worked out all these ideas into the glass. It's a meditation for me, the way I find clarity. When I'm done, I can see what I need to do. I need to face my father, and find out just what the fuck he means when he says he is dying. I lock up the studio and drive back to the hospital.

I think the staff is starting to recognize me. I get a smile from the receptionist when I ask for Ted Stag's room. As she prints out my visitor badge, I realize that a week ago, I'd be slipping her my number, making plans to go fuck her in a utility closet before getting on with my day. *Huh,* I think. *I don't even feel like doing that.*

It's surprising--this lack of an urge to block out the world with some meaningless sex.

I take the elevator up to the floor where my father is staying. Apparently they usually release him when he sobers up, but this time they say they've found some things and need to keep an eye on him in-patient. He's asleep, his yellow-tinged skin practically glowing in the hospital lights. I wander over to the nurse's station to ask for the Cliff Notes version of what's wrong with him, and someone tells me they'll page the doctor.

While I'm waiting, my brother Ty texts me a few times, but I don't even feel like I can answer his questions about our cabin trip. I'm worried I'll give something away, somehow reveal that I'm standing a foot away from the man who abandoned us.

"Mr. Stag? Dr. Stone." An older man approaches me with his hand extended. "I must say, it's a pleasure to finally see a loved one here with Ted."

I try not to snort. "He said he's dying," I say, shaking the doctor's hand.

Stone exhales. "These conversations are never easy. Can I get you something? Coffee?"

I shake my head. "Just lay it on me. What's wrong with him? Specifically?"

I spend the next half hour learning about advanced liver failure, and how the only cure is liver transplant. They can't put my father on an organ list because he's still actively abusing alcohol. Dr. Stone is stern when he meets my eye and says, "if your father can remain sober for six months, we could not only assess whether his liver restores function on its own in the absence of alcohol, but it can prove to us that he is serious about staying sober if he were to receive a transplant operation."

There's really nothing I can think to say in response to that, so I just sit and stare at the bed until eventually Dr.

Fragile Illusion

Stone pats my shoulder and excuses himself. He leaves me with his card and some info about a rehab program they recommend. He also hands me a pamphlet about living organ donation.

Twenty
EMMA

Tuesday, I wake up feeling energetic and sore as hell. I limp my way into work, hoping the walk will do me some good, but it's hard to concentrate. I'm thankful Phil doesn't have anything too complicated for me to work on. When I finally get home from work, I see a brown paper grocery bag on my stoop. My name is written on the bag in marker, with a note: *Hope this is the right size.*

I look inside and gasp to see a hand-blown coffee carafe. The bowl is clear with swirls of green and gold, and the thick, sturdy handle fits perfectly in my hand. I hurriedly unlock my apartment and, as fast as my aching, post-seizure body can move, hustle to the coffee machine, where I see that it is indeed the right size. I'm in the middle of fishing my phone from my bag to thank Thatcher for his surprise, when there's a knock at the door.

I peek through the window and see a sturdy-looking woman on my stoop, holding a folding table. "Can I help you?" I say, opening the door partially.

"Emma Cheswick? I'm Lucy, the massage therapist. Thatcher Stag sent me?"

Oh my god! This man not only makes me an artisanal coffee pot to replace the one I broke in nude shock, but he also sends me a massage therapist? The one thing in the world I really needed today but hadn't had an opportunity to arrange? *Is he for real?* I feel bad that my immediate thought is to wonder what he wants in exchange for all of this. I can't help but remember how he behaved when we first met, the sleazy, self-assured confidence that I was going to sleep with him in the greenhouse before his opening.

Lucy smiles at me expectantly, so I open the door for her. "I...don't know what to do. I haven't ever had...I didn't know Thatcher had hired you..."

"Don't worry about a thing!" she says, looking around. "I think I have plenty of room to set up in the living room. Give me five minutes and we can get started."

This gives me just enough time to fire off a text to the mysterious, ever-surprising Mr. Stag. **Are you for real with these gifts?**

You should make Lucy some coffee with your new, <u>fragile</u> pot.

Seriously, thank you, Thatcher. I don't know what to say here.

How about you let me come massage you instead?

Of course. Of course he wants to make this into some sex fantasy. **There it is. Pass.**

;) I'm kidding! But call me after.

I bite my lip as a thought forms. Before I can talk myself out of it, I type back **Just come over in an hour. We can eat the next meal from Alice.**

Lucy finishes setting up the table and soon, I am a blissed out puddle as her strong hands work out all the ache from my bones. We talk about my epilepsy, since it seems relevant, and it's so refreshing that she knows about seizures. Some of her clients suffer from them, too, and she knows just what to do to help me feel better. She pays special attention to my feet, which I hadn't even realized were bothering me until she starts to knead my arches. I could get used to this, for sure. When she's done, I pretty much roll onto the couch, guzzling water as per Lucy's instructions. I melt into the cushions, feeling my inhibitions slide away alongside my soreness. Thatcher knocks on the door and I holler at him to come in.

He laughs, seeing me sprawled out. "You look like you just smoked a bowl, Chezz."

"Mmm," I nod. "I actually have a meeting with my neurologist about that next week. There's a clinical trial at the medical school. For epilepsy."

"No shit?" His eyebrows fly up. He lifts my feet and sits down on the couch. My legs drape across his lap, and I feel the firm warmth of his thighs under my calves. He moves so casually that I hope he doesn't notice me squirm as heat

Fragile Illusion

floods my core. "I'd be down to help you with your research, Chezz. If you need someone to sample the goods and make sure they're safe, and all."

"Very funny," I tell him. I need to sit up and get my feet off his lap before I start stroking his crotch with my toes. I don't understand what's going on with my attraction to him right now. It's like my animal mind is attracted to his hot body and thoughtful favors, superseding my rational brain who remembers that he's a screw-'em-and-leave-'em kind of guy. Maybe this is just him working hard to get in my pants.

Before I can decide if that would be a bad thing, I stand up to reheat the next layer of Alice delights. "Asian stir-fry today," I tell him, reading from the label. "With coconut Jasmine rice. God, she's amazing."

"She definitely is," he says. Thatcher walks over to the island and winds his long, muscular legs around one of my stools. As I wait for the microwave I stare at his jeans. His thigh must be two feet long. My cheeks flush as I think about how easy it would be to reach over and just give it a rub. When he starts to talk again, I yelp a little bit, drawn out of my fantasy. "So I was hoping Lucy would grease you up so you'd be more amenable for my next big ask for Operation Fake Fiancé," he says.

"Hm?" I slide him a dish of stir-fry.

"I forgot there's a bachelor/bachelorette thing this weekend. My brothers, their ladies, and us, holed up in a cabin in Deep Creek."

"This weekend?" I set down my fork and pull up my calendar app on my phone. "Oh. Shit. Fuck. That's why Veronica was so pissed." Everything comes back to me with my sister dropping hints about our family dinner this weekend. "Logan and Veronica are getting engaged." I reach for my fork, take a big bite, and look again at the calendar. "What are the details of this Deep Creek thing? My mom's going to want us to come pretend we're excited for Veronica and her country club friends."

"That sounds fun," Thatcher says, grinning. "I can put a hoop in my nose. Your mother will love it."

I almost spit out my food laughing. "You're terrible," I tell him, sort of hoping he's not joking. We map out the logistics. He's going to pick me up from work Friday with bags packed. We will duck out of the Stag party early on Sunday, leaving enough time to get to the country club for Veronica's perfect announcement. I'm actually looking forward to bringing him with me. There's never anyone I feel comfortable around when I'm out with my family, least of all my perfect sister and her perfect degree in political science and her perfect relationship with my father's chief of staff.

Fragile Illusion

I feel sparks run down my spine when Thatcher's hand tucks a lock of hair behind my ear. "What's on your mind, Chezz?"

"Oh." I flush. His touch is really starting to affect me in ways I hadn't bargained for. "I was just thinking I am glad I will have an ally at this thing Sunday."

He smiles at me and his grey eyes are molten with...something. Can he be feeling this heat, too? I clear my throat and shift the conversation back to work, telling him about how excited everyone has been about his feature story and how much they're looking forward to reading about Juniper. "This weekend will really give me a chance to grill her," I tease.

Later, when he leaves and I sink back into the couch, I can smell traces of him. Spicy deodorant, the smoky smell of his workshop, and the lingering, wonderful scent of Thatcher Stag himself. **I think I'm in trouble,** I text Nicole. **I might be into this guy.**

Twenty-One
THATCHER

I have no idea what the fuck I am doing lately. As I drive home from Emma's place, all I can think about is the feel of her ankles. I picked up her legs and put them in my lap without thinking, like I'd been doing it for years, but when my skin made contact with hers, I thought my dick was going to spring out of my pants.

Her legs felt like warm velvet, her peachy skin soft and silky from her massage. I could barely understand what she was saying as we talked, because all I was thinking about was how badly I wanted her to rub her foot just a few inches higher up my thigh as she squirmed around.

When I go to bed, I dream about Emma, her red hair sprawled over my sheets, her eyes closed in pleasure as I lick every inch of her skin. I wake up with my dick in my hand, so close to release. Panting, I close my eyes again, imagining holding my weight above her body, plunging into her depths. A few strokes of my fist are all it takes to send me over the edge. I can almost feel her body grip around my shaft as I pump once, twice. I groan as a fountain of white-hot cum hits me in the chest. I lie in bed breathing heavily, trying to figure out what to do about this. I don't even know how to go after a woman when it matters to me if she turns me down.

I remember when my brother Tim first met Alice, how he told me she distracted him, how thinking of her made him do things he'd never consider, otherwise. I realize I can't call him to ask for advice about it, though, because he thinks Emma is already engaged to marry me. How stupid would I sound telling him I need to figure out how to get her to like me when we're supposed to be in love?

I have a meeting today with my agent about my next gallery show. I want to show her the new piece, but I feel suddenly private about it. Like I don't even want to display it. It's too personal, somehow. I'm still standing there staring at it on the shelf when I hear the studio door open. Cody walks in with Maria, my agent. He's looking scruffy as ever, dressed like me in jeans with an old t-shirt. Maria looks elegant in a blazer and slacks.

"Cody told me you have something new for the Warhol show," she says, practically jumping up and down.

"Cody should keep his fat mouth shut," I tell her with a sigh. I show her all the work I've finished since the opening at the conservatory, trying to avoid my private piece, but Maria sees it over my shoulder.

"My God, Thatcher. It's breathtaking." She reaches out a hand to touch it and I feel compelled to bat her arm away. I remember who I'm dealing with and catch myself in time, but

Maria sees the movement. "Hm," she says, "Feeling protective of this one?"

She steps back a few feet and looks at my work. "Something happened here," she says, pointing to the things I finished since Sunday. "What happened?"

"What do you mean?"

"There's a shift," she says. She waves her hand around at the shelf. "The energy is different here. Something changed about your work. And then we have this." She points at my piece.

I blush, and I'm shocked to be blushing, which makes me blush harder, until Cody laughs. "Thatcher's been hanging out with a woman," he tells Maria, and I kick him.

Maria's jaw drops. "The *same* woman? More than once?"

I shake my head. "It's not like that," I tell her. "She's...we're friends."

This draws a laugh from my long-time agent. She's been chasing down my work since I displayed it at an art show in high school. "You don't have female friends, Thatcher Stag. I've seen you. Women, for you, are for sex and, in my case, for brokering art deals." When I don't say anything, she plunks her bag on the table and sits on a stool. "So. Tell me what you know about Alex Clemont."

"The architect?" Alex Clemont is hot stuff right now in Pittsburgh. His name turns up in the buzz alongside every new restaurant opening, every new boutique...his eye for design is putting Pittsburgh on the map.

Maria nods and slides me a proposal. "He's in the middle of styling his new bar, opening in Lawrenceville. It's going to be a gin joint in some refurbished firehouse. He saw your work at the conservatory and wants two things." Maria flips the pages to a snapshot of some of my work nestled among the plants at the conservatory. "He'd like you to do something similar to this, looking organic and I believe he said the word 'flamey.'" I nod. I can meet with this guy and pull something together in a few days, and it'll finance my creative side ideas for the rest of the year. Maria continues, though, and I frown. "And he wants you to do a series of glassware for the bar. Stag Glass exclusives for gimlets and gin mojitos. Sturdy, but with that Thatcher flare."

I recoil at this idea. "I'm not a fucking Ikea, Maria. I don't do tableware."

She pats my hand. "Sweetheart, Alex Clemont comes around with this kind of offer about as often as you find a woman you talk to more than once." She slides the folder toward me and rises, walking toward the door. "Read it over and call me by Friday."

As we listen to the gravel crunch under Maria's tires outside, Cody snatches the folder from me. He scans the numbers and his jaw drops. "Jesus. Thatcher, come on, man. Look what he's offering."

I glance down, and then I sigh. I could have been making bowls and high balls for years if I wanted that. Hell, for awhile I made all my brothers beer steins every Christmas because it was easy and I could whip one up when I remembered at the last second. But that's not the direction I want for my work. Should I even consider this offer? Ever since all this...whatever this is with Emma, nothing makes sense.

I look back over at the shelves, trying to see what Maria saw about my work, how it's apparently shifted since last weekend. I realize, staring at a piece of dark green and black nodules inside a clear dome, that the day of Emma's seizure was also the day I saw my father again. I tell Cody I'll think about the Clemont offer, but now I have an idea for something bigger, something different. I chug a glass of water and get started.

Twenty-Two
EMMA

Nicole comes over after work on Thursday to "supervise" my packing for the weekend. I bubble on to her about my notes and outlines for the work I'm doing, and she pretends to be interested in my story ideas. Nicole always lets me talk at her while I'm in the brainstorming stage, and I never think she's listening, but she always has a comment that helps me move a story from blah to fantastic.

Today, she's definitely not listening, though. She's rummaging through my closet, grunting and huffing disapprovingly. "Emma," she cuts me off. "All you own are t-shirts and turtlenecks."

"Well, I have a cocktail dress for when my parents host events..."

Nicole rolls her eyes and looks at her watch. "Come on," she says, pulling my hand.

"Where are we going?"

"We have to get to the mall before it closes."

"Nick, stop. Come on. I don't need to go to the mall to go off into the woods with my fake fiancé and his brothers."

Nicole raises one eyebrow at me, marches over to my dresser, and pulls out a handful of cotton briefs, all a bit gray and saggy. "Ok," I say, "but so what if my undies are pathetic? It's not like anyone is looking."

"Did you not say he looked at you naked and commented on your pubes? Stop." She cuts me off before I can interject. "I am your best friend and I'm running an intervention on this saggy sports bra collection. Girl, not that I am trying to jinx this, but what if you have a seizure and pee your pants again? Do you want him to run into your suitcase and come out with a handful of Hanes?"

I mumble something incoherent, but follow her out to her car, and she drives to the mall. She grabs a giant shopping tote from the greeter in the department store and drags me to the lingerie department. We argue between the lacy, expensive selection and the practical, comfortable briefs, settling on some things that are functional, affordable, but sheer enough that Nicole stops rolling her eyes at me.

"Ok," she says, looking me up and down. "Now for a swimsuit."

"Oh, hell no," I protest. And it continues, but not for nothing is Nicole rising in the ranks at her company, landing investors and convincing top talent to come aboard. By the time she leaves my apartment that night, she has lightened my bank account, packed my bag for the weekend with the Stags, and left me more than a little nervous about what she's rolled into neat bundles in my duffel bag.

Fragile Illusion

Thatcher seems moody when he picks me up from work on Friday. His sullen demeanor leads me to chatter nervously about work, which feels weird to do with him since the subjects of my work lately are all related to him, or about to be. He pretty much just grunts periodically as he drives and I run out of things to say before we hit the state line.

"So," I say with a sigh. "What's on the agenda for this weekend? I should probably have asked before we were almost there..."

This he responds to, tossing an arm over the back of my seat and leaning his head against the glass of the driver's side window briefly. "Ty wants us to go for a run while you girls stay back and paint your toenails or whatever Juniper decides."

This makes me laugh. "I can't see Juniper choosing that particular activity..."

He finally smiles, and I feel the tension ease considerably. "No," he says. "She's not that type, is she, Chezz?" He tells me we will basically just be hanging out while Alice cooks her brains out without having to stop to take care of Petey. "He's back with Alice's dad and brother, having a man weekend."

The trip feels nice, familiar, comfortable, for a few minutes more, until Thatcher asks, "So, what if, you know, there's another seizure? This weekend? What do I do?"

My heart sinks. "I don't want to talk about seizures this weekend, Thatcher."

"Well," he protests, looking irritated, "I feel like I need to know what you can and can't do so you don't end up on the floor while we're in the woods far away from help or something."

"This is why I don't tell people. This. There is *nothing* I can't do, Thatcher Stag. You sound just like my mother, telling me I can't move away from home, can't attend classes in a brick and mortar school because of what *might* happen." He seems like he wants to interject, but now I'm pissed off. "I'm an adult, I take my medication, and the only reason I had a seizure the last time was because I didn't take my rescue meds. Because I didn't want to disappoint your damn sister and her special lime leaves."

He doesn't speak for a few minutes, but pulls his arm back to the steering wheel, holding it with two hands while we cross the border into Maryland. "Emma, I apologize for phrasing it that way. I know you're a very capable woman."

"Thank you."

He looks over at me and meets my eye, sweeping his long, dark hair back from those piercing grey eyes of his. In the fading light, in the shadows of his beard and long hair, he's all bright eyes and dark shadows. The tattoos on his arm blend together in the fading light until that looks dark, too. "Will you tell me if there's anything I should know?"

I sigh. "I take medications every day. I've told you--this is why I don't drink alcohol. If a seizure is coming, I can always tell, and then I should take my rescue medicine and sleep. I promise to tell you if that happens. Ok?"

He nods. "That's all I wanted to know."

"I'm just really sick of everyone in my life treating me like a baby," I say, looking out the window. Suddenly, I feel scorching heat on my thigh, and I look over to see him squeezing my leg through my jeans.

"I know you're no baby," he tells me.

I swallow, focusing on his hand on my leg, trying not to feel the pulsing heat, the burning desire for him to slide his hand a bit higher. "I just want someone to forget to be careful with me," I tell him in a quiet voice. When I meet his eye, there's no caution there. Instead, his hooded gaze is wild fire.

Twenty-Three
THATCHER

We are the first to arrive at the cabin, even though we stopped for snacks and supplies at the grocery store. I use the code Ty sent us to unlock, and step into the rustic space. There are high, vaulted ceilings with exposed wood beams, and the massive stone fireplace takes up one entire wall. I wasn't sure what to expect, but the cabin is furnished with deep leather couches, and the huge wooden table is set with candles.

Emma flicks a switch, and the whole place is aglow with twinkle lights inside and out. "Oh!" she gasps. "It's magical!" She wanders out through the sliding glass door onto the patio and I hear her exclaim, "There's a hot tub!" I laugh, knowing my brothers are going to drink too much and try to drown each other in there if we don't watch out.

I check my phone to read over the email from Ty, where he claimed the biggest bedroom for Juniper and him "because we're the fucking couple of honor," he wrote. Chuckling a bit, I peek into the next closest bedroom and toss my bag in the door. I feel Emma walk up behind me, and then she makes a small sound of surprise.

"There's one bed," she says.

I look over at her. I mean, I had assumed this, but I hadn't stopped to think that this would mean we'd be sharing. I suck

Fragile Illusion

air through my teeth for a minute and rub my beard, trying to think fast. I'm about to offer to sleep on the floor, but I see her collecting her wits. "Ok," she says. "We'll just build a pillow wall."

"A pillow wall?" I raise an eyebrow at her and grab her bag, placing it on the dresser.

"Yeah. A barricade. Because you can't keep your hands to yourself," she says, and without another word she starts unpacking her stuff.

Fuck, I think, seeing a glimpse of something black and sheer as she tucks her clothes into the top drawer. *I'm going to be in a bed with Emma.* I'm relieved when I hear my brothers pull up. They rode together because they came straight from the Stag Law offices where Tim and Alice and Juniper all work.

Soon, Alice is pulling out containers of dips and homemade pita chips, Juniper is mixing drinks, and Tim has even brought Emma a swing-top bottle of sparkling lemonade. When Alice plunks a sprig of fresh mint in her glass, they share a smile, and damn if I don't feel horny just looking at this woman fitting right in with my family.

Juniper brought a card game called Sushi Go, and soon, Emma and Tim are in a fierce battle for the win. Emma catches on really fast, and eventually, the rest of us stop really trying. We just want to watch Emma and Tim fight over sashimi and pudding cards. He starts yelling at her about tactics, and she doesn't miss a beat, dishing it right back to him, playing a defensive game. Emma isn't intimidated by Tim at all, and I love that. I catch Alice and Ty staring at her as Emma plays a card that causes Tim to throw his hand on the table and storm out the back door. Alice and Juniper burst out laughing while Emma tallies up the score. "Yes!" she says. "I beat him by 2 points."

I have to catch myself, because I want to kiss her for this, for beating my brother and pissing him off, but I know that would cross a line in our arrangement. Instead, I just smile at her silently, until I hear Ty and Juniper suggest that we help Tim cool off by throwing him into the lake.

Alice pretends to be worried at this idea, but everyone goes off to change into their swimsuits, leaving Emma and me sitting alone at the table. "You want to go change first?" I ask her. "I can clean up the cards."

She shakes her head and bites her lip. *Fuck*, I need to stop staring at Emma's lips. I want to lick them, and I really can't think that way. "I should tell you something," she says in a quiet voice.

"What's up, Chezz?" I put my arm around the back of her chair and turn sideways in mine, so I can lean close and hear what she's saying.

Fragile Illusion

"So, I can swim, and I haven't had a seizure aura at all, but...it's risky for me to swim. Unless someone is watching out for me." She pauses. Her eyes are watery, like it's killing her to have to talk about this. "Can you make sure I don't drown?"

"Of course," I tell her. I wink, to try to ease up the mood a little. "I won't let you out of arm's reach." Emma smiles and goes off to change into her suit, leaving me to put away the cards and think about long division or come up with some other strategy to keep my cool while I'm in the water close to this red head in nothing but a swimsuit.

"Oh my god, Emma! Your suit is so stinking cute!" I hear Alice fawning over Emma in the hall and decide it's safe for me to go back and change. My breath catches in my throat when I see her in a blue and white polka-dot bikini top with matching little shorts. She is so fucking sexy, all curves and soft skin.

When I walk out the back door onto the deck, I'm grateful for the low light of the twinkle lights along the dock. My brothers are already in the water, Tim past his hissy fit at losing a card game. Alice and Juniper are floating in an inflatable swan. Then I see Emma. She's lounging on a raft, just her legs dangling into the water. The moonlight catches her pale skin and she seems to glow, her red hair shining like flames even in the dark. When she looks up and smiles at me,

I'm gone. She has me totally under her spell and I don't fucking know what to do about it.

Then I see Ty swimming toward her while she looks at me, unaware. "No!" I scream, too late as I see him reach to tip her off the raft. Emma screams and flounders a bit. I know the lake isn't deep where she is, but I dive in and grab her.

I hold her against my body as she resurfaces, sputtering and panicking a bit. "My bad," Ty yells, treading water and looking sheepish. "I was just fooling around."

The lake water is slippery and warm, and Emma flails her legs looking for purchase. I keep one arm wrapped around her stomach while I move us toward her raft. I feel her body calm when she realizes I've got her, that she's safe. Ty keeps yelling his apologies while Juniper tries to dunk him and Alice rams him with the swan raft, scolding him for catching Emma off guard.

But all of that fades away for me as I realize that there's no hiding what I'm feeling right now. My body responds to Emma. I'm rock solid against her ass, even after she grabs the raft. She wriggles a bit in the water to stay afloat, but she stills, realizing that I'm hard as fuck. "Oh," she says, turning around to look me in the eye. "Oh."

"You ok?" my voice is low, my face close to hers. She nods. I feel her yearning for something, too, and I almost decide to lean in and kiss the hell out of her when my fucking brother cock-blocks me.

"Emma, are you mad?" His voice breaks the spell and Emma looks away, toward Ty. "I'm really sorry. I just wanted to treat you like one of the family."

"It's ok, Ty," Emma says, returning her gaze to mine. "But actually I'm pretty tired. I think I'm going to call it a night."

Her tone isn't one that invites me to join her in there, so I nod and stare at her as she climbs the metal ladder back up onto the dock. I don't even pretend I'm not looking at her ass as she reaches for a towel and then walks back up the ramp into the cabin. I float on my back in the lake, thinking about Emma rubbing up against me, Emma naked in the kitchen in the sunlight. I had sort of been turning off the part of me that goes right in for the fuck, knowing this thing with Emma has to hold together for at least a month. I really have no idea how to go about pursuing a woman slowly, maintaining a connection with her *and* fucking her. But shit. I want to fuck Emma Cheswick, and that's bad news. I need to stay here, submerged in the icy lake water until my dick calms down.

Eventually I climb out. Emma is long gone into our room, and Alice and Juniper are bent over some magazines on the deck, talking about seating charts for the wedding.

I sit up with my brothers a bit longer, drinking a few beers and bullshitting with them. When I go into our bedroom later,

I can barely see Emma asleep behind the barricade of pillows and blankets she's constructed in the middle of the bed.

Twenty-Four
EMMA

I wake up pinned under something heavy. I twist around in the blankets until I realize that my fortress of safety--every spare pillow I could find in the cabin--has all slid to the floor. The long, muscled, tattooed leg of Thatcher Stag is slung over my hip.

I roll over to look at him, trying to move his leg without waking him up. He's half on his side, sleeping in just a pair of shorts, and holy shit. I had forgotten the glorious sight that is his chest. His tattoos stop midway down his pecs, leaving his abs fresh and begging to be licked. *Stop it,* I tell myself. *This is a work weekend. You cannot mess up this arrangement with sex.*

The rational, journalist side of my brain who is just here to get information is struggling to overpower the aroused half of my brain who wants to run my nails down Thatcher's leg. My lizard brain keeps my eyes traveling straight down his abs to the huge bulge in his shorts. So it wasn't my imagination last night in the lake. Thatcher is packing a serious sword in his scabbard. I snort at my own joke, still trying to figure out what to do about being trapped under the long limb of this gorgeous, untouchable man.

Thankfully, I'm saved by the other Stags. Tim starts pounding on the door, yelling, "Thatcher! Get your ass up! We're going running in five minutes." He pounds a few more times for good measure, and I see Thatcher crack open one eye. He smiles at me, and I would probably fall over if I weren't already lying down. His grey eyes and dimples are dazzling, and I know he knows it. He looks damn good.

"Guess that's my cue," he says, rising from the bed and stretching. He faces away from me, so I'm forced to stare at his back muscles. The long hours of physical work shaping glass have done him a lot of favors--his body is exquisite. I'm staring, slack-jawed, until he bends over to put on his sneakers and socks, and walks out the door without looking back. "Coming, coming. You assholes better not leave without me!" he yells down the hall, and the Stag Brothers are gone.

I make my way to the kitchen, where Alice has set out an entire restaurant's worth of food. "Hey, Emma!" she sings, dancing her way between a griddle and a mixing bowl. "I'm making waffles. And eggs. And bacon."

"Gosh, Alice. Do you need help?" My eyes are wide, looking at the heaps of fresh herbs and vegetables, the little crock of fresh maple syrup she's set out on the table.

"Nope! Absolutely not," she says, sliding a mug of coffee down the counter toward me. "At work, I do all of this for about 50 people *and* I usually have Petey asking me 75

Fragile Illusion

questions per minute while I'm trying to concentrate. You sit and tell me about working at the *Pittsburgh Post*."

It's so easy to talk to Alice. When she asks questions, she really cares about the answer. She'd make a great reporter, and she blushes when I tell her so. I start to wonder what's going to happen after Ty and Juniper's wedding, when Thatcher and I are supposed to break up. It hadn't occurred to me that I would enjoy spending time with his family, and then feel sad saying goodbye to them. When he first told me he was fighting with them and blurted the lie about a fiancé, I assumed they were all stuffy jerks like my parents.

I can see how Tim is uptight, but I decide to ask Alice if she knows more about the fight that led to the ultimate deception. "This coffee is amazing," I tell her, breaking the silence as she stirs and chops.

She nods. "The guys at Zeke's roast the beans right in the city. I get a delivery at the office once a week. Hey." She looks up at me and brushes some of her wild curls out of her face. "Let me know if I get boring talking about food and farmers. Tim says people don't want to hear allll the details, but I get excited!"

I laugh and assure her I'll let her know if I ever get bored. "I'm a curious person," I tell her. "I wouldn't be a good reporter if I cut people off when they're on a roll!" We talk a bit more about her work, and I start to jot some notes in my

Lainey Davis

phone for the piece about the childcare they have on site. When we get to a natural pause in the conversation, I decide to just dive into the hard question. "What happened with Tim and Thatcher?"

Alice pauses and sighs. "You know," she says, "I'm not really sure. Tim was mighty angry that Thatcher was late to Petey's birthday party, and I think they just started to bring up a lot of years of held-in quarrels."

"I know Tim's opinion really, really matters to Thatcher. About everything," I tell her, looking out the window to make sure the guys aren't back yet. I see Juniper making her way up the steps to the back deck. She's wearing running tights and a sports bra and I nearly gasp when I see how fit she is. Her abs have abs.

She bursts into the kitchen and grabs a glass of water, chugging it down before she greets us. "Hey," she says, finally, heaving a bit. "I ran separately so the boys could bond and fight out all their shit."

Alice nods. "They really need to do that."

I look back and forth between them, puzzled. Juniper chugs some more water and continues, "They still haven't finished whatever they were getting into at the birthday party, and Ty thinks Thatcher is hiding something." She winks. "He hopes I'm going to get you to spill your guts today."

I frown, remembering that Thatcher had seen their father when he was waiting for me to change at the hospital. I guess he hasn't told his family about that yet. Well, I'm not going to be the one to bring that up. That's a hurt that runs years deeper than any of our involvement with this family. Then, of course, I realize that Thatcher is also hiding from them the fact that our relationship is pretend. I flush, realizing I'm part of this divide that's plaguing the Stag brothers.

"No worries, Emma," Juniper says, clapping me on the back. "Hey, anyone want to jump in the hot tub with me before the guys get back?" I tell her I'm going to stick to the house and Alice agrees to let me set the table at least. When the guys haven't returned an hour later, the three of us decide to dig in without them, and Juniper, fully at ease after her hot tub, really opens up to all of my questions.

Twenty-Five
THATCHER

Everything seems fine for about the first mile. My brothers give me shit about my new tattoos. I pretend that Tim is getting soft around the middle, and we all joke that Thatcher is starting to look like a shiny bodybuilder, his muscles are getting so big.

Then, Tim falls back beside me, letting Ty run on ahead, and I know it's all about to go down. "I read Emma's article about you," he says. "Why didn't you tell me you had a show at the Conservatory? I would have come."

I shake my head and keep running. "I did fucking tell you, Tim. I always tell you."

"When?" He seems genuinely shocked.

I just roll my eyes at him and speed up my pace. I'm not going to invite him to tell me I should really reach out to his admin if I want something to get on his master schedule. Somehow I doubt Alice has to do that, and my brother never misses one of Ty's hockey games. "I guess you don't remember shit unless it's earning your law firm money," I sneer at him.

By this point, Ty realizes we aren't in step with him and he pulls over beside a flat rock, panting a little bit. Tim stops running when we approach Ty and asks him, "Did Thatcher tell you about his art show at the Conservatory?"

Ty shrugs. "Probably? Was it in June? I can't be anywhere in June unless the team loses and--"

"I told both of you, like I always do. Neither of you assholes listens to me anymore because you've got babies and girlfriends. You've iced me out of your lives, but then you have the gall to get pissed off when I am late for one of *your* things. Fuck that."

I start running again, but Ty grabs my shoulder. "Don't run away, man. Let's talk about this."

"Fuck you," I snarl. "I liked you better when you just beat the shit out of anyone who pissed you off."

I take a step before I feel it. His fist is like a sledgehammer to my shoulder. *Finally,* I think. Then, I turn around swinging. Tim comes up to try to separate me and Tyrion, but years of scrapping have taught us both how to hit each other and how to avoid Tim's efforts to referee. I crouch low and aim for Ty's kidneys. He goes for my stomach every fucking time. Tim catches me in the eye with an elbow, so I hit him in the face, too. Eventually, exhausted, we all collapse onto the gravel path and just lie there, breathing heavy. I exhale long and slow through my nose and close my eyes. "Alex Clemont offered me a quarter million dollars to do a custom piece for his new gin joint and hand make all the glasses he'll need to serve."

"Is that the builder guy who did the fancy hot dog place downtown?" Ty asks, sitting up and stretching. I nod. "He does a lot of cool spaces."

Tim frowns and says, "Send your contract to Juniper. She's better at that kind of thing and can look at it for you."

A few minutes later, we turn around and head back for the cabin, the mood lighter. I know it's only temporary, though, because eventually I'm going to have to tell them I saw our father.

When we get back, the house smells amazing. I can tell Alice has outdone herself. She and Juniper are washing dishes and they both turn around, immediately swarming the three of us. Alice and Juniper see our cuts and bruises and get out the ice and soft hands, soothing Tim and Ty. I hear a lot of "poor baby" while they cluck their tongues. My blood is still pumping, and damn if I don't feel aroused after the adrenaline rush of fighting. I suck down some food until my brothers disappear into their bedrooms so their ladies can "check them out where there's better light."

I roll my eyes and grab a glass of ice water, clinking the cubes together in the glass while I slowly swallow. I walk softly down the hallway to the bedroom, looking for Emma, and I stop in the open doorway. Emma is perched on the bed, typing furiously. There's a far-off look in her eye while she writes and I can tell she's in the zone. Fully focused. Creating.

I chew on an ice cube, just watching her. She's so sexy, and I don't know if I'm just admitting it for the first time, or only letting myself concentrate on her while I'm agitated, but I want her. Badly. She's still wearing the too-big t-shirt she slept in, and it hangs low off one shoulder. Her red hair is piled on her head in a messy bun-thing, and I moan softly when I see that she's not wearing shorts. Just bare legs jutting out from beneath the laptop.

My cock springs to life as I watch her work, the way she nods her head and smiles when she must have found just the right word. Eventually, she clicks a few keys triumphantly and then clasps her hands under her chin, smiling. She looks so fucking happy right now, and I realize this is how I feel when I finish a piece in the studio. When I take an idea and form it into something solid, something real. Emma's words are her art, and it's hot watching her creative process. *Shit,* I think, watching her stretch, seeing her heavy breasts move inside the baggy shirt. *Fuck it.*

I crunch another ice cube, and she looks up at me, startled. "Oh," she says. "I didn't know you were back."

I close the door behind me and walk toward the bed, sinking down beside her. "Can I see what you wrote?" I set the glass on the night stand and lean toward her laptop, but she slams the lid shut and clutches it to her chest.

"NO!" she yells, surprising me with her ferocity. Then, she shakes her head slightly. "I never show anyone my drafts."

I raise an eyebrow at her, confused. "Why not?" But if I'm honest, I can guess why. Probably the same reason I don't discuss my designs or let anyone in the studio with me when I'm working. Hell, half the time I send Cody away if I'm deep into an important piece.

"It's like...it's too personal," she says. "It's private. It would be like seeing me naked."

I smile, remembering the sight of her in her kitchen. "I've already seen you naked, Chezz." I remember the feel of her body last night in the lake, the way she wriggled against my aching cock. I'm bursting with need for her. I slide the laptop out of her hands and set it gently on the floor beside the bed.

She sits sort of frozen, and I can see her chest rising and falling as she breathes, anticipating. She wants this, too. Her nipples are hard and I can see them jutting out through the thin material of her shirt. *Fuck me, she's perfect,* I think. "Come here," I say, huskily, and she closes her eyes for a moment, swallowing. When she opens them, her pupils are dilated until there's just a tiny ring of green around a sea of dark, wet black.

I lean back against the headboard and gently ease Emma onto my lap. She straddles me with those thick, bare legs of hers, and I groan as the weight of her settles against my throbbing hard-on. "I was watching you write," I say, moving her hips along my length. "You're so fucking sexy, Chezz. Do you know that?"

Emma emits a tiny moan and I know I can't stop until I hear her make that sound again, until I make her come and get to watch her face transformed by pleasure. I lean in to kiss her, pulling her close against me. I have one hand on her neck and the other on her ass, digging my fingers into the soft flesh, slowly inching that shirt up until I have a hand on her panties.

"Oh!" she exclaims, pulling back from my lips. "Your tongue is so cold."

Twenty-Six
EMMA

"You like that, Emma?" he asks, sliding his frozen tongue along my lips. Holy shit, do I like it. The heat of his body, the ice-cold of his tongue. The mix of sensations is like nothing I've ever felt before. My skin has been buzzing since last night in the lake, and now I'm finally connecting with Thatcher, touching him, feeling him touch me. It's sexy enough to be sitting on Thatcher's lap with his hands on my ass, but when he kisses me? I'm gone.

"Thatcher," I breathe, "I can't...work..." Alarm bells are ringing in my head. The ethics of what we're doing are already pretty terrible without me giving into some wave of lust. But then, I think about how long it's been since I've been with a man, and none of them ever touched me like this. None of them ever left me shaking with need.

I can't seem to find any words, and I just start moving my hips along his rock-hard dick. Last night in the lake, I thought he was maybe he got hard because he was embarrassed to have to rescue me or something, but now, his grey eyes are intense as he looks at me and thrusts his tongue into the far reaches of my mouth. He explores my mouth and his lips suck and nibble at mine. He's shirtless from his run, and I finally get to feel every firm inch of him. My nipples, achingly hard,

Fragile Illusion

brush against his through the material of my shirt. This is far and away the sexiest kiss of my life.

"I fucking burn for you, Chezz," Thatcher breathes, and I want to tell him I'm scorching, too. That I've been hot for him since he first pressed against me in that hallway, but I'm still reeling from the kiss, so I just sit there, panting. "Are you hot, too, Emma?" he asks, and then he looks at me, a devilish grin spreading across his sweaty face. He reaches onto the night stand and plucks an ice cube from his water glass. I gasp, nervous about what he's planning. His free hand slips down the back of my panties, his long fingers rubbing the sensitive skin of my backside. He lifts the ice cube slowly with his other hand, and I start panting when he presses it to my collarbone.

Slowly, deliberately, he drags the ice along my chest, up my throat, and along my jaw. He follows behind with his mouth, now searing hot, leaving a trail of opposite sensations that have my entire core on fire. I'm circling my hips, desperate for stimulation on my clit. He's torturing me with how good this feels. Thatcher puts the ice cube between his teeth, freeing his hand, and his cold, cold fingers slip down the front of my panties.

My shivers give way to frantic moans when I feel his icy fingers fluttering on my clit. "Jesus, Emma, you're soaked," he says, crunching the ice between his teeth before kissing me again. His tone is so casual, but there is urgency in his touch.

Lainey Davis

His fingers start to circle my nub inside my panties and I drop my head back, exposing my throat to him. Thatcher takes the opportunity to suck on the taut skin. "This feels so good, Thatcher," I moan. I am out of my mind, drunk on the sensations.

"Do you like this?" he asks me, sliding a cold finger inside me.

"Fuck, yes, Thatcher. Please."

"Please what?" he whispers in my ear, flicking his cold tongue along the shell. He never stops moving his hand on my center, teasing apart my wet folds. I can't even form thoughts right now and I struggle to answer him, but abruptly, he stops his movements. "Tell me, Chezz. What do you want?"

My mouth hangs open. I pant, my chest rising and falling. I reach behind me to strip off the shirt, baring myself to Thatcher, and I gasp, "Please make me come, Thatcher."

He laughs again and cups my breasts, the sensitive, soft globes filling his rough hands. His thumbs flick my nipples and I moan again as he says, "I thought you'd never ask."

I start sliding my palms up and down his chest, over the stag tattoo that matches the ones his brothers both have. I love the feel of his muscles shifting beneath my hands and I hunch down to lick one of his tiny nipples, enjoying the rumble in his chest when my tongue connects. I lick a salty path all the way up to his chin. And then I'm lost when I feel

Thatcher's mouth close over one nipple, sucking deeply, as he circles the other with another ice cube from his glass.

I drop my head back and groan in pleasure, no longer able to think when he switches sides, sucking deep pulls on the frozen nipple. He eases the melting ice back into his mouth and begins to slide his lips up and down my stomach, tilting me back, his hands under my shoulders supporting my weight, until his mouth has the access it needs to my belly.

He shifts his weight abruptly. Pulling me back against his chest, Thatcher kisses me again. I suck his tongue hungrily into my mouth, kiss his cheeks, frenzied in my need to connect with him physically.

His busy hands move to the waistband of my sheer panties, giving them a tug. "Can I see inside, Chezz?" I nod, and then yelp when he tugs them with both hands. I hear a rip as Thatcher yanks the ruined material off my body. "Holy fuck, Emma. Fuck, that's so hot," he says, running his fingers through the soft curls. "You're red *everywhere*."

My arms jerk and my back arches when he finds my slit. I might come if he touches me just once more. I'm trembling now as he takes his time exploring. "So wet, Emma," he breathes, sliding a fingertip just where I need the friction. Suddenly, Thatcher tips me backwards so I'm lying sprawled on the bed between his legs, looking up into his grey eyes. He grins his lopsided, devilish smile and reaches for the last ice cube. I gasp. He purrs, "You look flushed, Chezz. I want to cool you off." I'm frightened for a moment. Surely the ice on my most sensitive skin will burn? But then I feel the sting of contact paired with his scalding touch and I know I'm ruined for all other men. Forever.

"Oooh, ooh, shit, Thatcher. Yes. Oh my god," I start rambling and mumbling, fisting the sheets into my hands when he starts the agonizing, slow tease, sliding the ice cube up one thigh, then the other. He never takes a hand from my seam, and his fingers are cool from passing the ice between his hands. I feel my hips jerking involuntarily, a building sensation throbbing throughout my body.

Thatcher slides me back a bit further on the bed and bends forward. "Oh, god," I moan when he slides the ice inside me. There's just a small chip remaining, and the heat of my core melts it in seconds, but not before I come, hard, screaming his name and burying my fingers in his long hair.

I think he will stop when the sensation subsides, but he doesn't. He sticks out his tongue and licks me, over and over again while his long fingers massage my ass. His thumbs reach around my legs to stroke the skin of my upper thighs and his tongue thrusts inside me. "I can't, Thatcher," I yell, pulling his hair. My thighs slam shut against his ears when he starts to chuckle.

Fragile Illusion

He sucks my clit between his teeth, lets go of my ass, and spreads my pussy open with his fingers. He dives back into me, fucking me with his tongue. Before the first orgasm wanes, I come again, so hard that I can't tell where my body stops and his begins, and I lose track of the world. All that exists is this wave of pleasure that crashes again and again. Slowly, it subsides and I become aware that Thatcher has moved his head and hands away from my body.

"Emma," I hear him say. I open my eyes to see him kneeling above me. He reaches into his waistband, stroking his cock inside his shorts, and stares at me. "That was the hottest thing I've ever seen in my life."

Twenty-Seven
THATCHER

"Emma," I say, looking down at the goddess on the bed, all curves and softness and cream. She opens a green eye, her blissed-out expression gorgeous as fuck. Knowing I put that look on her face has me hard as glass, but I want more. "I have to make you come again."

"I need a few minutes," she says, reaching for my leg, one hand lazily exploring up and down my shorts. And then I remember something really fucking unfortunate.

"I didn't bring any condoms," I tell her, sinking down to the sheets so I'm lying beside her. Fuck, I'm so hard it hurts. It actually hurts. "Are you on birth control?"

"Of *course* I'm on the pill," she says, sharply. "But..." Emma looks at me, concerned. "Have you ever been...tested for anything? I know I'm safe..."

I lean in to kiss her, moaning when I taste those soft, full lips again. "I always use condoms, 100% of the time. And I got tested, really recently, actually." I kiss her again. "I'm clean."

She melts a bit in relief and closes her eyes again. "I trust you," she says, and with that I climb on top of her. I have to feel her against me. This is different from every other time. I've never even considered sleeping with a woman without protection, but suddenly I cannot imagine sex with Emma

Fragile Illusion

with any kind of barrier. Fuck me, I *have* to see her come again, have to feel it with nothing between us. I can't keep my hands off her pussy, the feel of that tight, wet tunnel capped with those amazing red curls. This is all new for me. Sure, the ladies have a good time when I'm with them, but it's never turned me on this much to make someone come. Taking Emma over the edge like that--twice!--was the sexiest thing I've ever done.

It's Emma's turn for busy hands, though, and I nibble at her neck while she searches my body, tracing the muscles along my spine and then yanking down my shorts. It kills me to separate from her body, even for a minute, but I draw back to get my shorts and my boxers down, kicking them across the room before I ease myself back on top of her.

I hiss when she grabs hold of my shaft, her small hand wrapped fully around me at the root. Christ, I fit perfectly into her hot little hand. She starts to stroke me just right and I'm worried I'm going to cum in her hand. "Chezz," I tell her. "You feel so fucking good right now. Your hands are amaz--"

"Thatcher," she says. I look her in the eye and she seems impatient.

"Huh?"

"Shut up and fuck me." Emma lines me up with her opening and she doesn't have to tell me twice. I sink inside her, letting out a deep groan as I fill her up. This is bliss.

Lainey Davis

Emma is hot and tight, slick with need, against the bare, sensitive skin of my cock. She moans and moves with me as I slide, slowly, in and out. I think back to her words from my truck. *I want someone to forget to be careful with me.* I know now that she doesn't want slow and gentle. She wants fire, hot enough to melt ice. I look into her eyes, touching my forehead to hers, and I slam into her.

"Ahhh! Yes!" she says, bucking her hips to meet mine. "Yes. Harder."

You got it, I think, pounding her body, but I can't even find words to talk. Emma is so wet, so tight. I can feel her squeezing my dick and she feels like home. Emma starts moaning into my mouth as I slam her mercilessly. I brace my heels against the headboard for leverage and redouble my efforts. My dick rams into her and each time I think I've gone too far, she claws at my shoulders and yells, "More, Thatcher! Fuck me just like this. Now!"

I start sweating, my weight balanced on my forearms. I look down and watch her tits jiggle with each thrust, and I feel savage. But Emma looks me in the eye with a fierce expression, and she's just as wild as I am. Her nails dig into my shoulders as she tries to pull me closer. She tilts her hips up against me, finding the friction she needs, until she starts pulsing against my cock. I can feel it before she even starts moaning that she's coming for me. Fuck, her face is beautiful when she comes.

"I'm going to cum, Emma," I pant out, and then it happens. I see sparks. My balls draw up tight and I explode inside of her, hot jets spurting out endlessly until I collapse on top of her. I feel Emma still throbbing around me and I kiss her. She holds my face with both hands, moaning into my mouth until her waves of pleasure die down. This is so different, being with a woman I know and, well, someone I care about, even as a friend.

"Holy shit, Stag," she says, breathing heavily. "I've waited my whole life for that."

Exhausted, I lower my upper body to the side of her, stroking her hair and letting her hold me. "For what, Chezz?" I don't want to move. Ever.

"For someone to fuck my brains out." Her eyes close. She's still breathing pretty heavy and I like looking down at the way her body moves as she breathes.

"You had sex before me, though? That didn't seem like your first time..." Panic surges through me at the thought that I was just rough and rowdy with a virgin, but Emma shakes her head.

"No. You misunderstand me. I've 'made love' before and had slow, gentle, boring-ass sex with men who asked me things like whether they should stop before I have an orgasm, because they were worried I'd have a seizure."

"Hmmm," I just sort of make a sound of displeasure. That hadn't occurred to me, but from the tone of her voice she didn't really like that level of caution during sex.

She wriggles out from under me and I feel a sense of loss when I slide out from her body. Emma props up on one elbow and traces a finger along the ink on my chest. "I'm saying thank you, Thatcher." She kisses my skin and the wet heat of her mouth makes my cock spring back to life. "Thank you for unleashing your inner beast."

I laugh as she runs her hands along my body. I take her hand in mine and guide it toward my dick, now standing straight up against my stomach again. "Chezz," I whisper into her hair, "I'll get wild with you any time that you want."

Fragile Illusion

Twenty-Eight
EMMA

After a blistering round two of riding Thatcher's cock while grabbing the wrought-iron bed frame for dear life, I feel both thoroughly exhausted and utterly embarrassed that his family likely heard me shrieking and screaming. "They're all going to know we were fucking in here," I whisper, hiding under the sheet once the sex-drunk euphoria begins to fade.

"Chezz," he says, tugging my hair, "They already assumed we've been fucking. We're engaged, remember?" I roll my eyes at him. Sex was never supposed to be part of our arrangement. I rub my fists on my temples, trying to figure out how to get back on track to professionalism. If that's even possible. Shit.

I rise from the bed, rummaging around the drawers for some clothes, and almost don't hear Thatcher ask, "What did you mean when you said *of course* you were on the pill?"

"Hm?"

"The way you said it, like I should know already. It's not like we had a lot of contraception chats when we got fake engaged..."

"Oh," I say, plunking back down beside him on the mattress. "To be fair I was a little distracted by all the orgasms you were handing out at the time." He laughs, pulling my hand to his mouth and kissing my palm. I'm stunned by the gesture, by the gentle feel of his lips beside the scratchier sensation of his beard along my skin. I pause and enjoy what he's doing. *So much for not mixing work and pleasure, I guess,* I think, before continuing. "The tone was me feeling like I have no choices about being on the pill. There's a correlation between seizure activity and hormone levels in a woman's cycle," I tell him, waiting for him to cringe, but he just looks at me, listening. "So I take a pill that keeps the hormones steady all month long. It helps, along with my other medications."

"I think all that shit is fascinating," he says, standing to put on his swim trunks. "The way they can know what might work to make your brain stop freaking out. Or whatever it's doing."

I nod, and then remember my own question. "While we're talking, can I ask you something?" He looks up from his duffel bag, where he'd been rooting around searching for something. "When did you get tested?"

"Oh," he says, biting his lip and looking out the window. "That was just last week actually."

I frown, assuming he'd gone to the clinic with the intention of sleeping with me this weekend. "So you just thought I'd jump into bed with you? What ever happened to your best behavior, Thatcher?"

He puts his palms up in surrender, saying, "Easy there, Chezz. Testing had nothing to do with you, although I never once let up hope that I'd convince you to sleep with me. Let's be perfectly clear about that." I make to leave the room, but he tugs on my arm. "I got tested because of my father," he says.

Wow, I think, sitting back down. "Ok, tell me more about that."

He flops next to me on the bed. "This whole fucking week, Emma. This whole fucking week has been so crazy. You had a seizure, I saw my fucking father, my agent got me a quarter million dollar project offer and--"

"Holy shit, Thatcher! You didn't say anything!" I slap his chest. "We should celebrate!"

He grabs my wrist mid-smack and pins my hand against his skin, and I can feel his heart racing. He's quiet for a minute, but says, "My father is dying. He won't get sober, so they won't put him on a transplant list. I started talking to the hospital about their living donor program." He looks at me, his grey eyes hard as steel right now. "That's when I got tested. For basically every disease that exists."

"Thatcher," I whisper, struggling to adjust my body so I can reach out to him, offer some sort of comforting gesture. He seems almost startled by that, so I extract my hand from his and pull his head onto my lap, running my fingers through his hair. "That's a hell of a week." He nods, silent, pondering, but relaxes into my touch. I take a deep breath, feeling way out of my element with this. Things have certainly moved beyond our little quid-pro-quo contract. "I think you should tell your brothers you saw your father."

I feel his body stiffen and I can literally feel him constructing an emotional wall between us. "I think you should stay out of my family business, Emma," he says, his voice cold. He rises from the bed and grabs a towel from the top of the dresser. "I'm going wash the sweat and sex off myself and then soak in the hot tub." And, in a few sharp strides, he's gone from the room.

Thatcher avoids me most of the day. Not obviously, but I can tell by his subtle shifts away from me or the way he abruptly tosses in a joke to steer the conversation away from anything related to his family. I don't know why I feel like I should meddle on this issue. I guess I feel partially responsible for him even being in this position. He wouldn't have seen his father at the hospital if I had done what I needed to and slept rather than go to his brother's house. *But then he'd never know about his father,* a small part of my consciousness reminds me. Surely questions are worse than working through a painful truth.

I bring my concentration back to the room, where everyone is hanging out and talking. Juniper and Ty picked up their marriage license. She starts telling a story about not having had parents and how that affects her when she's giving a health history, whether she's at the courthouse or registering for the Olympic team. I think about the tradeoffs for having parents that were involved in every, single aspect of my life. My mom was always so worried about my health that she never let me do anything. Always chaperoned every trip, said no to every slumber party invite until those faded away, and told me I was too fragile for every single after school activity, saying they'd all either stress me out until I had a seizure or else risk me getting hit in the head, triggering a seizure.

Over dinner of grilled steaks and roasted potatoes with corn on the cob, Tim startles the room by asking me about my medications. "I'm sorry," I tell him, looking up from my food. "Can you ask again?"

He dabs at his mouth with a napkin. "I was wondering who your neurologist is and whether you're participating in any new trials for epilepsy." Everyone stares at him, because Tim has never casually asked me a question. He shrugs. "My college alumni magazine had an article about some new research for seizures."

I nod. "My doctor is Dr. Khalsa and yes. Everything I'm on now has been part of his research, since I started college." I tell them how my big act of defiance against my parents was applying for a room and board scholarship so I could live on campus and finally get out from under their thumb. Once I moved into the dorms, my roommate, Nicole, learned about my epilepsy and dragged me to the student health center. She'd read a case report for one of her intro classes, studying Dr. Khalsa and the business angle of the medications he developed. I look around at all the Stags and Juniper and they're fascinated by what I'm saying. Not concerned or pitying--interested.

It's been so long since I've told anyone about my condition--not since human resources when I got my job. I'm really not used to people who don't flip out and treat me like I'm some fragile flower about to wilt.

So I keep talking, blushing a little bit as I explain that after my seizure at Alice's barbecue, Dr. Khalsa invited me to try a study for medical marijuana. Thatcher perks right up at that. "I forgot about that, Chezz." He waggles his eyebrows at his family. "Now you really know why I'm marrying this girl."

I shake my head. "I can't share with you. That'd be unethical--and illegal. I haven't decided if I'm going to do it, anyway."

Tim nods, contemplating. "I wonder what the ramifications are for medical marijuana use for, say, professional athletes...I mean it's legal in this state for certain conditions..." Alice swats his hand and tells him to stop thinking about work while we're on vacation.

As she rises to clear the table, Tim stands to help her. I meet Thatcher's eye and try to signal that I think he should tell his family. "Tell them," I whisper. "They deserve to know."

Thatcher's gaze turns dark and he shakes his head, his eyes holding me to silence.

Twenty-Nine
THATCHER

We all swim in the lake again after dinner, but Emma keeps her sexy ass as far away from me as she can. I know she's pissed that I'm not telling my family about finding Ted Stag on his deathbed, but fuck if I'm going to bring that up two weeks from my brother's wedding. He should be focused on his bride, on starting a life and a new family with this woman.

I sigh and think back to fucking Emma this morning. I'm not used to the idea of sticking around--I do *not* do relationships with women--but I definitely want to go at it again with her. I need to get her to stop being mad at me first. Maybe knowing we have an expiration date makes sex with Emma feel more comfortable. Not comfortable. Explosive. Searing. Addictive. *Fuck.* I'm forced to float on my back in the water and stare at her, remembering the look on her face earlier when I made her come with my tongue and, later, my cock.

Juniper wants a Sushi Go rematch after the sun sets, but I try to send signals to Emma to wrap things up early so we can go to pound town again. She seems oblivious, and kicks my foot away when I try to stroke her calf with my bare toes. I was kind of a dick to her all day, but I know I can make up for it. I make a point of rattling the ice in my glass, making eyes at her over the top, but she scowls. All right, enough of this shit.

"Emma, can I talk to you for a second?" I rise from the table and head toward our room.

"I'll be back in just a few minutes," she says, not moving her eyes from her hand of cards. "I'm about to kick Tim's ass again."

I feel myself getting angry, and that just pisses me off further. This is why I don't get into relationships, damn it. I don't understand what's pissing her off right now, but I know it all definitely changed since we had sex. I kick the bedpost in our room, yelping when my bare foot connects with the iron. I'm hopping around howling in pain when Emma comes in, crossing her arms and looking pissed off.

"What the hell is with you, Emma?" I hiss, sitting down to rub my foot.

"What the hell is with *you,* Stag? You give me the silent treatment all day, refuse to tell your family that you're thinking of giving a major *organ* to your father, and expect me to keep this secret from them all?"

"You have no problem keeping the fact that we barely know each other and are pretending to be engaged a secret," I whisper-yell at her. "I gave you the scoop you needed to keep your job, and now you have the access you need to my family for these other articles, so mind your fucking business. Play your part."

Her eyes flare at me and she puffs out her cheeks. I can tell she wants to deliver an earful, but is trying to contain herself. We stare at each other for a few minutes until she says, "I'd prefer it if you slept on the floor tonight."

"Fine!" I throw all the pillows from the bed down onto the braided rug on the floor. I yank off my shirt, grab the quilt from the trunk at the foot of the bed, and flop my ass on the carpet. She huffs out of the room, I guess to finish her card game, and I pretend to be asleep when she comes back a few minutes later.

I close my eyes and listen as Emma gets herself ready for bed. She turns off the light and we listen to each other breathe until I eventually fall asleep.

In the morning, Alice sends us off with a huge cooler of snacks and sandwiches, as if it's a six-hour drive to Emma's parents house instead of an hour and a half. Tim tells me to give Senator Cheswick his best and I grit my teeth when he asks if I can slip him Tim's card. Emma looks fucking amazing in her fancy dress for this country club party. She's even wearing pearls. She looks me up and down--I told her dark jeans and a button down with wingtips is the most I'll nod

Fragile Illusion

toward that square lifestyle--and I can't tell if she approves or not, but she sniffs and hugs Alice and Juniper.

Ty gives her a high-five, then pulls her into a hug. I stand leaning against my truck with my arms crossed while the five of them act like they've known each other a lifetime, and are parting ways forever more. "Emma," I say, "We don't want to be late for your sister's thing."

She waves and climbs into the truck, her good mood fading as the door slams shut. After a few minutes of driving, she says, "Ok, we need to make a plan for today."

"I plan to deflect every question to you, Chezz," I tell her, shifting into fourth gear and letting the sound of the tires on the highway drown out her voice. By the time we pull into the party and I toss my keys to the valet, I think there can't possibly be anything colder than Emma's mood. And then, of course, we encounter her parents.

Thirty
EMMA

"I accept your apology, Veronica." After the nightmare at the country club, Thatcher dumped me and my things on the curb and peeled off in a snit. All I want to do now is sink into a hot bath and then go to bed. "Yes, I understand that you had planned this announcement with Logan a long time ago. I never intended to upstage you. Thatcher and I were trying to keep things quiet until after his brother's wedding, like I said."

From the second we arrived today, my family picked at Thatcher. To his credit, he smiled and politely deflected every barb. I flush with pleasure again remembering my mother asking him where she might have seen his "little creations," since he's an artist. Thatcher smoothly asked her if she'd ever heard of the Museum of Modern Art. Did it with a straight face, too. She fluttered her hands around and promised to look him up later.

But Veronica threw an absolute fit. She grew louder and louder, hissing and screaming that I sprung some edgy, artist fiancé on the family on purpose just to detract from her big moment with Logan. And my father chimed in that he didn't think my "engagement" was a good tactical move for his re-election campaign. The wait staff actually had to come to our table and ask Veronica to keep her volume down.

Fragile Illusion

"Veronica," I interrupt her asking me if it's absolutely necessary for Thatcher to wear a nose ring to her wedding. "I have a meeting with my neurologist in the morning, so I need to get some rest." Talking about my neurologist always gets my family to shut up immediately. They hate that they didn't select this doctor for me from their approved list of big names, but they do begrudgingly recognize that his help has improved my life dramatically. We hang up the phone after she offers another half-assed apology for letting her manners slip away in public. Because, of course, in private the other Cheswicks think it's fine for my family to judge people and make decisions about my love life based on how it looks for my father's campaign. I set an early alarm and flop angrily into bed, wondering how I'll smooth things over with Thatcher.

I spend the morning writing from home and submit a draft to my editor, who is giving me comp time for the afternoon since I "worked" this weekend. Around 3, I take the bus to the hospital and run into Dr. Khalsa in the lobby, which surprises me. He must be really excited about this medication trial. "Ah! Emma! There you are." He takes my arm and introduces me to his colleagues. We walk to one of the conference rooms rather than his office, where he sets up a presentation and starts to explain their new clinical trial on medical marijuana.

There are tons of questions from the International Review Board and a hell of a lot more paperwork than I signed when I started taking my other medications. Those actually alter my brain function. Isn't this a bit much hoopla for some pot? After about an hour of this, Dr. Khalsa asks me if I'd like him to go with me to the dispensary to pick up my "medication" for the trial.

"Um, sure?" This is hands down the most bizarre experience of my life, up to and including the time I covered the Furry Convention for the *Post* and had to interview guys who get their rocks off dressing like foxes and squirrels. We walk a few blocks to a standard-looking office building and take the elevator to the Wellness Center. When we walk inside, the space looks like a spa, with potted orchids and sleek, modern furniture.

I thought it would be skeezy, reminiscent of the pot dealers I visited with Nicole in college. There's not a Bob Marley poster or tie-dyed tapestry in sight. There are tablet devices on the wall for people to go "shopping," and Dr. Khalsa explains that we don't need to use those because I need to use very specific products for the clinical research. An employee greets Dr. Khalsa warmly and takes us back to a small, private office. Instead of chairs, we sit on yoga balls while the staff explains that I'll be using a vaporizer and cartridges that come pre-filled.

Fragile Illusion

They slide me a slim device that looks like a compact mirror...but Dr. Khalsa explains that I simply slide the cartridge inside, press a button, and inhale the vapor. Eventually, the goal is for me to no longer need my standard medications, but Dr. Khalsa has me on a graduated plan for his clinical trial. All the cartridges are pre-filled, ready to go. "Just follow the schedule, and I will see you in two weeks for some testing," he says.

I feel my jaw drop when the cashier asks me if I saw the discount for Shark Week, but Dr. Khalsa explains that I'll be using the hospital's account. I am assigned a number, and everything is taken care of by the researchers. Dr. Khalsa even arranges for a car service to take me home, so I don't have to sit on the bus with my medication. I know he's just feeling antsy about me getting pick-pocketed, but I'll take a ride where I can get it.

I ease into the back seat of the sedan, enjoying the leather interior and air conditioning on full blast, and I pull out my phone to a series of missed calls and texts. Nicole, of course, is eager for details from this weekend.

A text from Phil: **This draft is tolerable, Cheswick.** Definitely nicer than when I submitted my last draft. I think I'm really solidifying my spot on the staff. I squirm in my seat a bit, anxious to get to work tomorrow and see his comments for revision on my article about Juniper.

Lainey Davis

Then a text from Thatcher. **Can we talk?**

I chew on my fingernail. I know I need to see him. We left things...tense. I tap back *Want to come over? I'll be home in ten.*

C u soon. Will bring sandwiches.

One thing I am really coming to like about the Stag family is they always have food. *Door will be unlocked. Just come in,* I write back.

When we get to my apartment, I tip the driver and settle into my couch to re-read the instructions on the "vape" pen. Because of my condition, and how much it sucks to have seizures, I never experimented with drugs or alcohol. Once I found out what works to keep me healthy, that's always felt more important than a temporary buzz. If I'm honest, I'm glad Thatcher is coming over later to be here after I use these cartridges. I have no idea how my body is going to respond. I finger the medic alert bracelet that's always with me.

Reading through the information sheet one last time, I decide I'm ready. I slide the cartridge into the pen, press the button, and breathe deeply. I feel the cool vapor swirling into me, and I slowly exhale. Not bad. I try again. *Hm.* Now I guess I just wait. I whip out the log from Dr. Khalsa and record two puffs, 4pm, Monday. No seizure aura today. Feeling great.

I set the supplies on the coffee table and wait to feel...different. Nothing happens except I have to pee, so I make my way into the bathroom, slightly disappointed.

Thirty-One
THATCHER

"Knock-knock," I yell, feeling weird just walking into Emma's house, even though she told me to. I hear water running somewhere in the apartment, so I walk in and sit down on the couch. I drop my messenger bag filled with takeout sandwiches, and look around. I love that Emma keeps the glass I gave her in a prime spot where it gets the sun. It's the focal piece of her entire apartment, and I smile, knowing she's thinking of me basically any time she's looking around her living room. I also definitely see now how she thought I made her a neuron.

The afternoon light catches the sculpture, and I follow the line of reflected light to the coffee table. "Hey now," I say to myself, seeing what Emma's got: an entire bag full of cartridges from the dispensary and...yep. A loaded vape pen just sitting on the table, begging me to try. *I brought this girl sandwiches,* I think. *She can spare a hit.*

I breathe in the smooth vapor, realizing Emma has acquired some seriously high quality THC. I'm just exhaling it all through my nose when Emma opens her bathroom door and sees me using her shit. She looks pissed.

"What the fuck, Thatcher," she shrieks. "I told you that's from my doctor. I'm not allowed to fucking share that!" She

Fragile Illusion

throws a shoe at me. Honest to god, reaches down, takes off her shoe, and throws it at me. I duck. "It's illegal and..." she grunts and throws the other shoe, "It's going to mess with Dr. Khalsa's results."

I set the vape pen down on her table and stand. "Emma, Jesus, I'm sorry. I took one hit." I pick up one of her shoes and hold it out to her, and she stares at it, laughing hysterically. *Oh, so she's already stoned.* I meet her eye and draw back, like I'm going to throw the shoe back at her. She squeals and fumbles around, reaching for the bookshelf.

"Thatcher Stag, don't you dare!" Emma yells.

"How do you like it, Chezz?" I toss the shoe at her, not hard, and both of us laugh when it hits her in the boob.

She gets closer and nails me with a book. "Will you knock it off? Fuck!" She hits me in the head with a hard back, and I stride across the living room to block her. When I get close, Emma yelps and starts running away with a copy of Harry Potter book 7. "Oh no. You're not throwing that at me. That's the heaviest one." I catch up to her in the hall and reach for the book. She's holding it up high as if I'm not almost a foot taller than her. But rather than snatch it easily from her hand, I decide to tickle her armpit.

She shrieks and tries to run again. *It's on now.* I can definitely feel a buzz, which makes this whole thing even more hilarious as I chase her. We're both laughing now. She tries to

Lainey Davis

slam her bedroom door in my face, but I block her with my foot, wiggling my fingers like a tickle monster. Emma trips on a pair of shoes and goes to the ground. I drop on top of her, dodging a spike heel, and start to tickle the fuck out of her.

"Damn you, Stag," she grunts, kicking at me, but then she starts laughing a deep belly laugh when I find a sweet spot on her sides. She keeps on laughing and I pin her arms above her head with one hand, using the other to lift the hem of her shirt. I meet her eye, and then drop my head to blow raspberries on her stomach.

The sound of Emma laughing is probably the most magical thing I've ever heard, or maybe the vape cartridge was just that good. Soon I'm lying on top of her and Emma stops laughing when she feels me grow hard against her stomach. She breathes heavily for a minute, searching my face, for what I'm not sure.

I smile at her. "You ever fuck someone while you're high, Chezz?" She shakes her head. I drop one hand to her tits and squeeze. "You want to try it out?"

She lifts her head to take my mouth in a fierce, possessive kiss. I respond in kind, thrusting my tongue in and out of her mouth, hard, while I reach up inside her shirt to find her nipples. I fucking love how she feels under my hands, helpless with her arms pinned above her head, and loving it.

Fragile Illusion

She moans as I circle one rosy nipple with my thumb, so I release her arms and get both hands on her sensitive tips. There's no finesse to how she's moving now. She's desperate, needy. I can tell her nerve endings are firing like crazy and I love seeing Emma unhinged like this. "Thatcher," she breathes, the sound of my name on her lips the biggest turn-on since I saw her naked for the first time.

Her hands fumble with my t-shirt and waistband, like she can't figure out which to take off first. I sit up to help her out, reaching behind my neck to strip off my shirt with one hand. "Ahhhh, shit," I hiss, as Emma dives into my jeans. She pulls out my shaft and gives my balls a squeeze. I look down as Emma climbs to her knees and drops her head into my lap. "Oh, fuck," I moan, as that pink tongue darts out and circles the tip of my cock. "Emma, holy shit. That feels so good."

I kneel on the floor of her room while Emma sits in front of me, sliding her perfect mouth along the length of my shaft. She's got one hand at the root of my cock and the other massaging my balls. This is an art form, a fucking thing of beauty. She looks up at me with those big, green eyes, her red hair tumbling all over her face, sticking to her sweaty cheek, and then she slides me so far into her mouth I can feel the back of her throat on my tip. I groan and drop one hand to her back, gently rubbing her, while the other rests on her head. I don't ever want this to stop...until I realize that I might blow my load in her mouth, and I haven't gotten to fuck her yet. "Emma, sweetheart, you gotta stop," I say, and she pulls off my dick with a wet-sounding pop.

"Or what, Stag?" she says. "What will happen if I don't?" She teases me like she's going to dive right back on to my dick, but I can tell she's playing with me now. I grab hold of her waist and spin her around until she's on her hands and knees on the floor.

"I'll fuck you from behind until you scream, Emma," I whisper into her ear as she moans. "That's what." I yank down her slacks and panties, pulling them just past her knees. I haul her up so she's on all fours and reach down to her center. I find her wet and hot, swollen and ready for me to slam inside her. "You want me to fuck you now?"

She nods, and I slide a finger inside her. "You're soaked, Emma. What's got you so wet?" I tease her, withdrawing my finger as I kick off my jeans and boxers. I kneel behind her, massaging her round ass, giving it a shake.

"Thatcher," she groans. "Please. Fuck me, Thatcher."

And there it is. With that permission I grab hold of her hip and drive inside her. Emma screams, delighted, and I wrap my other hand into her ponytail. I love how my fingers look entwined with the fire of Emma's hair. She bucks her hips back against me as I pound into her. I can feel my knees scraping on the floor and I know I'm going to have brush burns later, but I don't give a fuck. I've got an incredible woman wrapped around me right now and I don't ever want to let her go. The realization of that scares me for a minute, and I slow down.

Emma looks over at her shoulder, her eyes hot with lust, her mouth hanging open until she bites her lower lip. I meet her eye and redouble my efforts. She starts breathing heavier and lifts one hand, moving it to her clit so she can get herself off. "No," I growl, surprising us both as I push her hand out of the way. "I'm going to make you come, Emma. Me. I fucking love to make you come, Chezz," I say as I bury my hand in her red hair. One above and one below. I rub one of my thumbs along the back of her neck, and I rub the other in slow circles along her throbbing clit.

As Emma starts to moan, I drop back onto my heels, pulling her onto my lap so she's bouncing up and down on my cock. Lowering my hand from her neck to her chest, I feel her tits shake in my hand while she rides me. "I'm so close, Emma." I'm panting as I pull her against my chest. "I need you to come for me." And for probably the first time, she does what I tell her to. Emma starts to moan and I feel her pulsing around me, milking my dick until I blast off inside her.

"Emma!" I shout her name, pulling her in tight until the lightning stops, until the thunder of my orgasm quiets down and I can see again. Together, both of us gasping and slick with the sweat of exertion, we tumble to the floor in a knot of red hair, Emma's jeans, and wet pleasure from both our bodies.

Thirty-Two
EMMA

"Is this what drunk feels like," I ask, one hundred years later, entwined in Thatcher Stag so tightly I can't quite figure out where each of my limbs is located.

"No, Chezz," he says, laughing at me. "This is what stoned feels like."

"Hmmmm," I sigh. "I like this." I think I drift off to sleep, but eventually I open my eyes to see Thatcher kneeling beside me with the hand towel from my bathroom. I hear it dripping on the floor. "Did you just soak my towel?"

He starts to giggle. "I couldn't find a wash cloth, but I wanted to clean you up," he says. And the gesture is so sweet, that I try to let go of my frustration. I spread my legs a little and let him wipe me, slowly and gently. The warm cloth feels good along my thighs, along my center. "Mmmmm, that's nice," I say.

"Do you know how hot you are, Emma Cheswick?" he asks, and I shake my head. "You're the most amazing woman I've ever seen." He drops to his knees between my legs and plans a kiss on my clit. Suddenly, I'm wide awake as he shows me just how much he likes what he sees in me.

My skin feels like it's been electrified. Every inch of me is tuned in to what Thatcher is doing in a totally unique way. I feel laser-focused on his tongue and the way it slowly laps at my folds, the way his thick fingers slide inside my body. This is what it feels like to be worshipped, and I am loving it. I come quickly, taking me by surprise, and I groan his name, pulling him up by the shoulders until his head is close to mine.

I reach out a hand to touch his beard. He's glistening with moisture. *Me,* I realize, touching the hair beneath his lower lip. "Mmm," he moans as I slide my thumb along his lip. "That's right, Emma. You're dripping wet for me." He kisses my neck and slides a finger inside me. "So." Another kiss. "Wet." Another. "Just for me," and he slides inside me, fully sheathed. Our hips touch and I open my mouth wide.

"I'm so full, Thatcher. So full of your cock." And then I can't think, can't form words as he thrusts, hard. I have no idea what I'm doing with my limbs, but I see myself wrap my legs around his waist, dig my fingers into his shoulder. I cling to him, not wanting any separation from our bodies, as he grunts and, just as I shatter into another orgasm, he fills me with his own sticky release.

By the time Thatcher brings the sandwiches into my bedroom and we tuck in, breaking all my rules about food on my sheets, it's dark outside. He hands me a huge glass of water and tells me it will help with my dry mouth.

Fragile Illusion

"How did you know it was so dry???"

He laughs. "This isn't my first time getting high, Chezz." I tell him I'm glad he's here, since I have no idea what to expect, and he says, "I'm like your weed doula."

"What the hell is a doula?"

He talks with his mouth full, wiping his wrist over his lips, explaining, "Alice and Amy hire these ladies who help them out when they're in labor. So it's like...someone who helps you do hard things. Anyway, it was a joke."

Weed doula. "I like it, Thatcher. There's not a lot of people I trust to help me do hard things." And damn if Thatcher Stag doesn't blush a little bit when I tell him that.

He finishes his sandwich and rolls on his side, looking at me. "We need to talk about the thing with my father," he says, his expression stern. I nod. "I'm going to tell my family. All of it. But I'm not going to tell them before Ty's wedding," he says. "I don't want to give Ty the burden of having to decide if he wants him there or not."

I furrow my brow. "Wouldn't he want his father at his wedding? I mean, doesn't he want that now, regardless of whether you found him?"

Thatcher shakes his head. "He wants a dad at his wedding, someone who raised him and cared about him and wants to see him happy. That's Tim. Ted Stag walked out on us when we needed him most."

"And...so you're just going to give him an organ? Undergo an invasive, risky surgery? Because why?"

He flops back on the bed. "Jesus, Emma, I wish I hadn't told you. I didn't say I was going to do it, ok? I said I asked about it. I got some testing. I still don't even know if I'd be eligible, but--" he drifts off.

"But what, Thatcher?"

"But it has to be me if it's going to be one of us. Tim has kids and Ty is a professional athlete. It matters more if something happens to them."

"Thatcher!" I sit bolt upright. "Do you mean to say you don't think it *matters* if something happens to you during surgery?"

He exhales long and slowly. "Look," he says. "I just got a huge fucking contract. I can live off that money for a few years, at least! The way I see it, I can complete the work for Clemont, have the surgery, and take my sweet ass time recovering. I'll even be able to float Cody's salary while I'm laid up."

I stare at him with my mouth hanging open. "You were going to just go through with that entire plan and not involve your family? How would you feel if they did the same thing," I ask.

He closes his eyes. "I'm going to tell them. After the wedding. I promise." And he rolls over, snoring in my bed before I can even decide if I want him to spend the night.

Thirty-Three
EMMA

I can't muster up the energy to leave my room, but I'm also not ready to fall asleep yet, so I stretch, reach for my phone in the heap of clothes on the floor, and call Nicole.

She picks up immediately. "Listen, my so-called friend. You have kept me waiting for like 36 hours to hear about your weekend with the Reindeer. This better be good." I can tell Nicole is still at work. If she's at home, her voice echoes off her nearly empty apartment walls.

"You know it's Stag. And anyway, you can't yell so loud your co-workers hear, Nicole." I hear her chair creak as she adjusts her seat.

"Yeah, yeah. Spill it, Ems." I sigh. "A sigh like that? Shit, I should get some ice water."

"Funny you should mention ice," I tell her, and proceed to fill her in on the wild, mind-blowing sex I had with Thatcher.

"So he gave you an orgasm before your first orgasm was done...orgasming?"

"Pretty much."

"Jesus, Emma. Can I have a ride when you're done with him?" I know Nicole is kidding, but it doesn't sit right with me. I don't like the thought of Thatcher with someone else. I frown. "Your silence is very telling, friend. Want to tell me more about that?"

I look over to Thatcher's sleeping form. He's rolled onto his stomach and one long arm dangles off the edge of my bed. He's so tall that his toes peep out from the bottom of my blankets, suspended in the air, making me giggle. "He's here right now, Nick. I, like, texted him for sex and he brought sandwiches, and I thought he'd leave after, but now he's asleep." I blurt it all out so fast that I don't have time to hold anything back.

"Hmm," she says. "I'm going to have to meet him. I need to see how he acts around you."

Usually, I don't move ahead with a guy until Nicole gives him at least a thumbs sideways, but I feel sheepish at the idea of asking Thatcher to meet my best friend. "I don't know..."

"Let me know the next time you're going to see him and I'll at least give you a ride. Before he gives you a ride." She bursts out laughing so loudly I look at Thatcher, making sure he doesn't stir. "Seriously, though, Emma, I'm really glad you found someone who gives you hot sex. You deserve some hot sex. Never settle for mediocre sex."

I sigh. "I see that *now*. I really had no idea. Did I tell you Dr. Khalsa has me doing a trial of medical marijuana?"

"Jesus! I'm coming over. Wait. You have a naked man in your bed. Shit. When am I supposed to hear all about this??"

Lainey Davis

Once I get Nicole to calm down I am able to tell her how Thatcher stole a hit from my "science weed" as she calls it. "I still can't believe some dude got to see you for your first high. I've known you for years! Can I watch you get high tomorrow?"

"Of course, Nick." We share a laugh and plan for her to come to my apartment tomorrow evening. Once we hang up, I realize there's nothing left to do but crawl under the covers with naked Thatcher, and try to sleep. I try to ignore my sense of longing for him to drape that inked-up arm over my shoulders.

Thirty-Four
THATCHER

I open my eyes to see what's tickling my face. I know I have long hair and a beard, but I don't usually half choke myself on my own locks. Then I remember. I fell asleep at Emma's after two rounds of, frankly, the best sex of my life. When I turn my head, she's there next to me in the bed. Her red hair is sprawled everywhere. Thick and straight, it has strands of gold, brown, and umber. I can't help myself--I reach out and start to run my fingers through the silk, stroking it and watching the colors shift in the light. I look at the contented smile on her face and, rather than feel eager to get the fuck out of here, I feel so damn glad to wake up beside her. I was supposed to be talking with her about our exit plan for this contract. I need it to be her who breaks things off, or else the whole thing was pointless. But right now, ending things with Emma is the farthest thing from my mind.

My stomach growls and I decide to comb Emma's cupboards and make us some food. That's what a real fiancé would do, right? Might as well play the part since I'm here anyway. I slip on my boxers and dig through the fridge. She doesn't have much, but I figure I can make French toast at least. I get to work and am just sliding the first slices on to a plate when I see Emma padding down the hall wearing my t-shirt. I freeze as a huge, unidentifiable emotion seizes my chest. It's not arousal, although I definitely feel turned on looking at her with no bra, imagining her pink, tight nipples pressed against the fabric of my shirt. I frown, realizing that I'm feeling some combination of possession and pride and, well, joy at seeing her like this in the morning. Limping a little, smiling a lot, looking content.

"You cook?" her smile is dazzling. I'm glad I decided to do something nice for her, if it means I get to see that look on her face.

I shrug. "When I'm hungry." I drop a piece of toast onto another plate and then slide it down the counter toward Emma. "You've got a hitch in your giddy-up, Chezz," I say, grinning when she winces climbing onto the stool.

"Well, whose fault is that?" She takes a bite of toast. "Mmm, this is really good, Thatcher. Did you add cinnamon?"

I nod, turn off the burner, and sit in the stool next to her. I nudge her with my shoulder playfully. *What the hell am I doing?* I haven't flirted like this in years. I don't need to. Women are usually throwing themselves at me, and I always know I'm going to go back to their place. Emma is different. I care what she thinks about me, and she calls me out on my bullshit if I act like a jerk. I made her breakfast, for fuck's sake. I clear my throat and get to the matter at hand. "So,

Emma, like I said, I think we need to make a plan for, you know, after Ty's wedding."

She frowns and puts down her fork. "How am I supposed to break up with you? I'm not doing it in public or causing a scene at the wedding, let's be clear about that."

"Jesus. No. You don't even have to actually do anything. We just need to agree about what we're going to *say* you did. Will do. Whatever." I finish my toast, thinking. "You know it has to be you ending it, right? We talked about that."

She nods, pushing her fork around in the puddle of maple syrup on her plate. I think for a bit, sigh, and tell her, "I think it can work if we just tell my brothers your parents don't approve of me. Which is true anyway."

Her jaw drops. "Thatcher Stag, I would never end a relationship with someone because of what my parents think! No. Absolutely not!"

"Emma," I put my hand over her hand. "This isn't about what you would *really* do. Remember? This is about convincing my family that I'm not an oversexed playboy."

"They're going to think I'm some frivolous child who does whatever her parents want her to do!"

"Well who cares what they think of you?"

She recoils from me, staring. "Are you serious? This whole thing is about you caring what they think of you, Thatcher." She sighs and stomps off to the bedroom.

"Hey," I chase after her. "Come on, Emma." She throws my jeans at me.

"I have to go to work, so you should probably get dressed and take off. That's your M.O. isn't it? Morning meeting? Busy day ahead?" She yanks on a pair of jeans and a black t-shirt, throwing my shirt back to me before she slides her feet into a pair of Toms. "Look, Thatcher, thank you for the great sex and the breakfast. I don't accept your proposal for this ending to our illusion, but I'll think on it and get back to you in a few days."

"My proposal?" I fish around under her bed for my shoes. Shit, this gives me a sense of déjà vu.

"Yes. This is a business transaction, right? I'm negotiating our exit clause. But first I'm going to go meet with my editor and you're going to leave my apartment and do whatever it is that you do."

I'm used to women being angry when I leave the morning after sex, but I'm not used to feeling like I want to make things right. This shit with Emma is screwing with my head, because she's supposed to just be someone I'm making a deal with, and now everything is complicated and layered. I shake my head and rest a hand on her shoulder for a minute since I feel like kissing her, but know that she'd probably slap me.

When I get in my truck I pound the steering wheel a few times. "Fuck!" I shout in the empty cab. This is why I don't do relationships. Even when it seems like it's just fun, it always gets intense.

Before I can check myself, I aim my truck toward downtown and pull into the visitors lot at the hospital. I'm in a foul mood, and I feel like telling my father a few things about how fucked up it is to leave your family when they need you. They moved him to a private room on a different floor. The nurse in the hallway tells me he's getting released soon and they're hoping someone can convince him to check into a rehab center now that he's been safely detoxed.

I don't greet him, just walk in and sit in the chair beside his bed. He drops the newspaper he's holding and turns to look at me. "Didn't think I'd see you back again."

"Yeah, well you were asleep the last time I came. So now I've been a better son to you than you deserve. Twice."

He closes his eyes, then looks at me. "I want them to let me die, Thatcher. I can't do this without Laurel."

I want to feel bad for him, that he's so wrecked about this, but it's not like my brothers and I weren't wrecked, too. "Fuck you," I spit out. "You had responsibilities. To us. You think she'd want you to treat us this way?"

He just shakes his head. I feel depleted now, so I stand up and shove the chair away and walk out of the room.

Thirty-Five
EMMA

Phil calls me into his office first thing to talk about my draft. I submitted a profile of Juniper, highlighting her journey to Olympic gold while also transforming the law office where she works. Stag Law used to just focus on *male* professional athlete contracts, but Juniper helped them expand to represent women's sports and other equity issues. Now Stag Law has a huge, national reputation as the go-to firm for equal rights or equal pay cases. They even handle cases for people who need legal protection based on their sexuality. I closed the article by describing Juniper sitting for the bar exam in various states, years after she finished law school and initially took the exam, so she'd be able to serve clients wherever they need.

Phil, of course, wants more. "Needs more grab," he tells me, sliding the marked up copy across the desk. That's it. The extent of his commentary. I interpret this brief speech as him sending me back into the field, which is how I find myself riding the elevator up to Stag Law to shadow Juniper at work for the day.

She greets me with a hug at the elevator and ushers me directly to the kitchen, where Alice is getting ready for lunch. "Can't talk now," she says, stirring a giant cauldron of something delicious-smelling. "I'll ring the bell in an hour and you can sit with me and Juniper and dish!"

I feel awkward accepting their friendship after Thatcher and I just tried finalizing plans to end things. But I had agreed to play the part for two more weeks. I wonder if there's a way to break up with Thatcher but still hang out with his family? I follow Juniper to her office, where the walls are decorated with pictures of her on the podium in Tokyo. I pause in front of a picture of her with Ty. She's got a gold medal around her neck and is beaming straight at the camera. Ty just looks at her, his face utterly transformed by love and pride. He's got an arm around her shoulder, squeezing like he never wants to let go. *I want someone to look at me like that,* I think, drawing a ragged breath.

"So," I ask her, sitting down opposite her desk. "What are you working on this morning?"

Juniper smiles and spins her laptop around. "I know I shouldn't," she says, "But I'm looking at wedding stuff." She's got a Pinterest board open with different ideas for favors and programs. She bites her lip, waiting for my response. I'm touched that she'd show me something so personal, so obviously important to her.

"You're quite a complex person," I tell her, scanning the different pictures.

Juniper says, "I want to do something that celebrates hockey and rowing...I mean those are really the things that are important to Tyrion and me...none of these templates have quite what I want."

"You know," I tell her, digging into my bag for a card. "Some of the graphic designers at work do this kind of thing on the side for spare cash." I find what I'm looking for. "I bet if you hit up Hillary she could lay out a program for you in a few hours."

"Really??" Juniper claps her hands. "This is the very last thing we have to really do before the wedding. That would be amazing." She snaps up the card and closes her laptop. "Ok, whew. Enough about that. Now we're going to drive over to the football stadium and yell at some offensive linemen who got a drunk and disorderly the other night."

A few hours later, and I know for sure I have Juniper's story rounded out. I can't wait to get back to my revision. I want to show everyone this amazing woman I've met, who can man-handle 300-pound football players and, in the next breath, navigate a settlement with a university who refused to offer equal scholarship funds to the women's varsity rifle team. By the end of the day, Phil agrees they can run the piece a few days before Juniper's wedding. He claps a hand on my shoulder. "Nice work, Cheswick," he says with a smile. "This

Fragile Illusion

will generate the kind of buzz we need, and it's writing that's got meat to it." He stands up from his desk, grabbing his bag. "I'd offer you a drink, but you don't do that. So I'm sending you home early to celebrate...however you do that sober."

I can't believe my boss said "nice work" to me. I'm doing really creative writing, interviewing interesting people and getting feature-length assignments in the biggest newspaper in the city. It's like a dream come true! I immediately text Nicole to see if she can get away for a bit.

When I get to her office, she's in the middle of an intense game of foosball with a group of colleagues. I lean against the wall, watching. I love how Nicole takes no shit from anyone, elbowing some guy out of the way when he tries to offer advice on how she can get more leverage. She sinks a goal and pumps her fist. "Yes! All right. Now, I'm taking a break for two hours. I expect that proposal on my desk when I get back, guys. I'm serious."

She drapes an arm over my shoulder and we walk out into the warm July sunshine. "Friend," she tells me. "We are going to get ice cream, and then buy you a dress for this celebrity wedding, and then you promised I could watch you get stoned." I laugh, relieved I can trust Nicole to help me find a dress my mother would hate, but will make me feel comfortable in a room full of lawyers and professional hockey players. "Do you think you can hook me up with any of those

Fury hockey players?" she asks while we wait for our waffle cones. "I need to have some sex that has me limping like you, girl."

Fragile Illusion

Thirty-Six
THATCHER

Emma doesn't call for a few days, and then texts me out of nowhere, demanding a ride to family dinner on Sunday. Ok, she didn't demand. But I don't even know how the hell she found out about the dinner, unless she's been texting with Alice and Juniper. If that's the case, then I am well and truly screwed when it comes to ending this whole thing. Sure, sex with Emma is amazing. But then we always end up in a fight and it's too much work to make peace. Now she's hanging out with my sisters in law. They're getting way too friendly. It's starting to feel like an actual relationship with Emma, and that's a lot of work I'm not interested in doing.

I'm cold and distant when I pick her up, and I can see by her face that she's pissed at that. I'm not even sure why, but I really dig into her and say, "You didn't have a seizure aura today did you?"

She whips her head around to glare at me. "No. What makes you ask that?"

"You're acting like something crawled up your ass and bit you," I sneer at her, knowing full well she's just responding to my bad attitude. I don't even know why the fuck I am picking at Emma. Probably because I had a shit week after seeing my father, a shit meeting with my agent, and now I don't feel like playing pretend at my family dinner.

Emma just sighs and stares out the window. I must be acting like a dick if Emma Cheswick doesn't even feel like fighting with me. Fuck it.

We get to the house and Emma disappears with Alice and her sister. Amy looks a little bit like she's going to explode, but I hear her tell Alice she still has 3 weeks left at least. I try to remember what Alice looked like pregnant with my nephew, but that draws up a memory of my mother, swollen and round, pregnant with Ty. I don't have the space to be thinking about my mother today so I head out back to the cooler where Tim keeps the good beer.

I don't even pause to appreciate how it tastes. I work on drinking it quickly until I hear my younger brother coming toward me. "What's eating you, Thatch?" Ty is Mr. Good Mood, sauntering shirtless into the back yard.

"Why the fuck do you look like that?" I gesture at his mesh shorts and sweaty hair.

He shrugs and cracks open a beer. "Juniper and I ran here."

"From Washington's Landing? What's that, like 3 miles uphill?" I chug the beer even faster now. Literally everything is pissing me off today.

Ty sips his beer. "Four and a half. We went around the zoo. Hey, man, take it easy." He sticks out an arm to slow me as I open a second beer, but I shove him out of the way. I down it and grab a third. Used to be, the three of us went running together every Sunday and then ate pancakes with our grandma. Now Ty runs with Juniper. Who even knows if Tim leaves the house anymore. I've been running alone.

When I get back inside, Alice's brothers are watching baseball on the couch, so I sink in next to them and try to ignore everyone until it's time to eat. I'm feeling just about buzzed enough to calm down after 3 beers, but everyone definitely stares at me when I take a seat opposite Emma instead of next to her.

The table creaks under the weight of 12 sets of elbows, and I focus on the scratched wood, precariously heaped with corn, tomatoes, and grilled chicken. Eventually I become aware that someone is talking to me when there's a lull. "What?"

Emma clears her throat. "I was just telling them that I got a new assignment to interview the director at the Center for Organ Research. The national headquarters is here in Pittsburgh, and they're going to talk to me all about organ donation."

"That's fucking morbid, Emma." I shove a forkful of chicken into my mouth. I know I've hurt her. She's so interested in everything, always wants to research different

Lainey Davis

things and learn more until all her damn questions are answered.

She narrows her eyes at me. "Well, some things are morbid, Thatcher."

Tim makes a face and puts down his fork. "Our mother was an organ donor," he says. We all stare at him, and Emma, sitting beside him, puts a hand on his shoulder. What the fuck is going on here? She has no right to be comforting my brother about our dead mom.

"Nobody wants to talk about organs and dead bodies over family dinner," I grunt, emphasizing family and glaring at Emma. She pulls her hand back into her lap and raises an eyebrow at me. "Why don't you ever write about anything pleasant?"

"Oh, like a smarmy ladies man who sticks glass in the gardens?" Emma tosses her napkin down on her plate. Ty and Tim stare at us, but I don't say anything. Fucking Emma keeps going, though. "Thatcher might be an interesting source for this piece about organ donation," she says to the room at large.

Ty pipes up, "Why would anyone care about Thatcher for a story about that?"

I shake my head and kick her under the table. *Oh fuck. Please, shut up, Emma. Fuck. No.* But I'm not fast enough. She blurts, "Because he's looking into the living donor

Fragile Illusion

program." I guess this is how she responds to me being rude on purpose. By airing out my shit to my nosy family.

I breathe slowly through my nose, trying to hold my shit together. I want to throttle her right now. "I can't fucking believe you, Emma."

She stares at me and I glare back at her.

"What's all this?" Tim is in full dad-mode now, leaning forward past Amy, who starts to interject about all the living kidney donors she treats at work and how great that is.

Amy looks at me. "Are you donating a kidney to someone?" She looks back at Emma, who is red in the face and shifting in her chair uncomfortably. I hope she feels bad now that she's stirred up the Stag family drama.

"I think you should leave now, Emma," I say, my voice cold. My family all stares at me. I'm going to have to hash it out with them now. They won't fucking ease up until I tell them everything, and I am furious.

Emma just nods and stands up. She stumbles a little walking toward the door, and Alice runs over to her. "Emma, wait. How are you going to get home? Tim will drive you."

"Alice," Tim says, his eyes on me, his voice flat. "Call Emma a car service. I think my brothers and I need to have a talk." He stands from the table, throwing down his napkin and gesturing toward the garage out back. The Petersons all cough uncomfortably and Alice's brothers keep eating, but Ty stands up. Sighing, I follow them out back. Might as well face the music.

Ty shoves me against the wall. "The fuck is wrong with you, talking to Emma like that? And why the hell would you get angry-drunk at family dinner?"

"Enough," Tim says, crossing his arms, staring at me like he used to when I came in at 2am on a school night. "Tell me what the hell is going on. Leave nothing out."

An hour later, Tim screams at Ty to put a shirt on and he drags us all into his Volvo. "Where the hell are we going?" I sneer at him from the back seat. He just grits his teeth. I know full well he's driving us to the hospital.

"We're going to confront him," Tim says, "and tell him we hope he dies a slow and painful death, and that he is absolutely not risking your life to take one of your fucking organs, Thatcher."

"It wasn't his idea," I say. "He doesn't even know I met with the counselor about it." I had gotten my results back earlier in the week and I am a perfect match for my father, in perfect health.

"Tell me again what your plan was here, bro?" Ty grabbed another plate of food from the house and is eating in Tim's car, swatting his hand away when he tries to take the messy food. "You were going to get the money for your project and then, like, get your body parts chopped out and rest up for a year?"

"Something like that."

"At what point were you going to inform us of this master plan," Tim spits out. "Did you think we would just not notice when you showed up with a cane and a giant scar?"

"Do you really think you would notice, Timber?"

"Fuck you, Thatcher." He slams the car into park and starts walking toward the entrance. We follow him, the three of us slowing down as we approach the room where Ted Stag is fully unprepared to see us en masse, for the first time in 15 years.

He drops the book he was holding as the three of us stand in the doorway. Tim grinds his teeth, seeping fury and pent up rage. Ty looks like he's going to cry, taking deep, heaving breaths. Our father looks back and forth at the three of us, our mother's grey eyes staring coldly back at him. I know we look intimidating. Hell, we were intimidating as kids. We're grown ass men now, all over 6 feet tall, and pissed as hell. Our father speaks first. "Good to see you again, Timber. Should I kick *you* out of *my* space this time?"

"What is he talking about," Ty asks, shoving his hands in his pockets.

"This asshole tried to crash your party," Tim says, not breaking his stare at our father. "After your first game with the Fury. I had him ejected."

"What?" It's my turn to feel shocked. Our sanctimonious brother saw our dad and never fucking told us? And somehow I'm a dick for keeping secrets?

"If he can't be there when we need him most," Tim grits out, "he doesn't get to be present when we celebrate."

Ted Stag swallows and his head flops back against the bed. "I suppose that's fair." He looks out the window. "Thatcher told you this is it for me?"

Now it's Ty's turn to speak up. "He fucking told us you have an opportunity to get sober."

Dad scoffs. "You think I want someone's liver? You think I'd take that? Would you want your mother's liver to go to me?" Tim recoils like he'd been shot. God, now I'm thinking about who got our mother's organs, who got to use her final gifts.

"Ok," Ty says, his voice shaking. "So you don't get a second chance at life. But don't you want to spend your final days sober? You only get one fucking life, Dad. You think Mom wouldn't fight like hell to enjoy every second of this?"

"Your mother was always better than me," he says. "In every way." A tear rolls down his cheek, but I can't drum up the energy to feel bad for him.

Fragile Illusion

A few minutes of tense silence pass before I place a hand on each of my brothers' shoulders. I lead them into the hallway and, as soon as we're in the elevator, I pull them in for a group hug. For a long time, we just hold each other, not speaking, communicating everything and nothing all at once.

Thirty-Seven
EMMA

I tell Tim's driver to take me to Nicole's office, where I collapse on her couch in a heap of tears. Nicole shouts for an intern to bring me soup from their kitchen and I marvel through my sobs at how different life is inside a tech startup.

"I blurted his secret," I moan to Nicole. "And now he's so angry at me!"

She furrows her brow. "Weren't you scheduled to break up with him in a week anyway? Sounds like fate took that out of your hands..."

My eyebrows rise. "But...it wasn't supposed to be this way."

"What way, Em? Did you think you'd become fuck buddies and then make your silent exit and never see each other again with no hard feelings from either side?"

"Yes!" I shout, burying my head in my hands. My nose is running but I'm too upset to wipe it up. "No! I don't know."

Nicole slides onto the couch next to me and puts her arm around my shoulders. "Honey," she says. "It's ok to have feelings for him."

I shake my head. "He doesn't do feelings," I insist. "Have you seen him on the Internet? He's a cold-hearted snake."

She pets my hair, speaking softly and comforting me. "It sounds like he's just defensive because the people he cares about keep dying or walking out on him."

Nicole urges me to go home and take an extra puff on my vape pen before climbing into bed. I notice she's got a copy of the Post on her desk and I sob again when I see that my story on Juniper is on the front page of the Sunday edition.

Over the next few days, I leave Thatcher five texts and two voicemails, trying to apologize for blurting his secret to his family. I've stopped crying as hard about it and start remembering how he was such a dick from the moment he picked me up that day. In fact, he had been rude to me since the morning after we last slept together, so maybe it's not me who needs to be in apology mode. Well. Anyway we both messed up sort of equally.

What would a relationship with him be like? Constant fighting probably, his moody outbursts. Me always worried about blurting the wrong thing to his family members...*Or maybe he'd always bring you just the right food and make you come until your eardrums burst,* I think.

I spend the week trying as hard as I can to get over Thatcher Stag and our fake, amazing-sex "relationship." I'm on the verge of getting there when my mother shows up at my apartment Wednesday evening. After I let her in, she stands in the doorway, sniffing uncomfortably as she looks around my home. She's only been here once before and it's better for both of us if she doesn't stay long. "Emma," she says, lifting one eyebrow at me while I microwave the dinner she interrupted. "You know your sister has *such* a lovely little home in the southern suburbs. There's a direct train line to downtown..."

"My office is on the North Side, mom," I say, trying to keep emotion out of my voice and focus on the facts. "I'd have to transfer."

She sighs. "Well, anyway, I've come to make sure you have an appropriate dress to wear tomorrow evening." When I look at her, confused, she points to a stack of mail on the coffee table. "Your father's fundraising event is tomorrow. I made certain to inform you via email and by post, as this one takes place in your...neck of the woods." Because of the weird way that voting districts are mapped out, my father's constituents mostly live in the wealthy suburbs south of the city, but there's one small panhandle that reaches the north side of the city. I'm actually surprised he hasn't hit me up to do more campaign propaganda for him before this.

"I've been busy with work, since the hospital and all..." I wave a hand at the stack of mail. It's a total lie. Work has been amazing. At home I'm just wallowing in sadness that I messed things up with Thatcher.

My mother frowns. "I hope you haven't been giving too much of your time to that man you're calling a fiancé."

I sniff. Then I sigh and roll my eyes. "Give me the breakdown about dad's thing."

She smiles. "It's in an art gallery! Andy something."

"Dad's having a fundraiser at the Andy Warhol museum? I'm impressed. He must really be courting edgy voters." I start to slurp at the frozen soup I nuked for dinner. I don't invite my mother to sit, and she doesn't.

"Yes! Well, voters are voters, dear. There are a number of artists whose work is being displayed, and they'll be present, mingling with donors. It's going to be a very impressive evening."

I make a face at my mother. "You know artists do things like pierce their noses and grow long hair, right?"

She clucks her tongue. "I'm certain that's only the low level artists who aren't *used to* the notoriety that can come with pricing their work at this level." She sniffs and her nostrils flare. "This will be a *sophisticated* event. I'll expect you there at 6pm. Dress is cocktail attire, Emma."

She swirls out the door just as my phone vibrates with an incoming message. I snatch it up eagerly, hoping it's Thatcher, but my heart sinks when I see it's from Juniper. **The programs turned out just perfect! Can't wait to show you Friday night at rehearsal!**

Lainey Davis 201

I feel like I shouldn't even respond until I hear back from Thatcher. I don't even know if I'm still supposed to be going to the wedding with him. Maybe the explosive Sunday dinner was the ending to this whole charade after all.

Thirty-Eight
THATCHER

Maria paces around my workshop with me, helping to select the final piece to stick in the new showing at the Andy Warhol museum. It's a big fucking deal to have a piece in that museum, and I know that, but I'm so wrecked emotionally that I can't get it together to micromanage my display. Thankfully Maria knows her way around my work and the look I am shooting for. She's got Cody boxing up my new series of green glass. I'd been melting down old beer bottles and adding in bits of cobalt, sculpting ephemeral looking shapes. Lots of swirls. People are into swirls these days. I like them, but Maria frowns, walking past, tapping her fingers against a clipboard.

She walks over to the shelf where I keep my Emma. I'd been calling the piece she inspired my Emma. I stare at it for hours each day, trying not to think about her, but unable to look away. I know I need to call her, talk to her. I haven't seen my brothers since Sunday, either. Just been holed up in my studio working at the furnace nonstop.

"This one," she tells Cody, reaching for Emma.

"No. That's not for sale." I fly off my stool.

"Thatcher," Maria looks at me, puts her hands on her hips, and scowls. "You don't need to sell it. You just need to *display* it. This is the fucking Andy Warhol museum."

I shake my head vehemently. "Not that one. That one's private, Maria. I told you that last time."

"I remember. And I disagree with you." She turns to Cody and insists he box up the piece. "We'll display it in the center of the green glass swirls. I like how they go together."

"If you so much as chip it, Cody, I'm going to pull out your teeth one by one." I start pulling my hair, which reminds me that I promised Ty I would trim my hair and my beard before his wedding. *Just make it so it looks deliberate,* he'd said. He really did ask nicely, and I make a mental note to visit the barber. Anything to keep my mind off all this shit with Emma and my family.

When Maria and Cody take off with my glass, I feel unsettled. I don't like being in the studio without my Emma. I think back to how I was feeling the day I made that piece, how I'd just come from sitting with her in the hospital and then taken care of her like it was nothing. And it was nothing--it felt as effortless as taking care of my nephew. I do that for family. Not anyone else, though. It's too risky. Safer to just keep everyone distant before they get a chance to walk away from me when I'm an asshole. The thing is, Emma isn't going away. She left me a bunch of messages this week. I'm the one who isn't calling back. It's me not letting her in. I keep telling myself if I ignore her, she will go away and I can focus on my art in peace. Just how I like it.

Only today I can't find any fucking calm. My refuge is buzzing. The empty space on the shelf makes me uneasy, and I don't want to be in here anymore. I close up shop and drive over to find my brothers. I can be near them even if we're all mad at each other.

Tim's office is closest, and I'm surprised when I run into Ty at the reception desk. Then I realize he's probably there to fuck Juniper on her lunch hour. I'm not sure why that pisses me off, but it seems like everything irritates me this month. "Thatcher," Ty yells. "Good. You saved us a trip. Come on."

"Where are we going? What's going on?" Tim walks into the hallway, adjusting his tie as I see Alice slink out of his office, smoothing out her work coat.

I snort. "Jesus, Tim. Can't you guys do that at home?"

He coughs and mutters something about the childcare at work, and then turns on Ty. "What was so important I had to leave my meeting early?"

"Your meeting? Come on, man."

We ride down the elevator and pile into Ty's new Range Rover. "You like?" he asks. "Juniper bought it for me as a wedding present."

"You two are ridiculous," I mutter, punching Tim's shoulder since he made me sit in the back seat. "Where are we going?"

Ty sighs. "I don't want to get married and start a new life with JJ until we hash shit out with dad."

"Nope," I say, pulling on the door, which unfortunately locked when Ty put the car in gear. "Not going with you for that." I jiggle the handle to no avail.

"Fuck you--I have it on child lock in case Petey rides with us," Ty says. "This is what I want from my best men. I want us to go together and tell our father to go to hell, but also I want us to invite him to clean his shit up and maybe stick around. Meet his daughters in law and grandkids someday."

For the next hour, I remain silent. When we get to the hospital, Ty tells him exactly what he said in the car. Ted asks questions about Tim's wedding band, waves around Emma's article from the Post, asking about Ty's wedding this weekend. I roll my eyes. "You don't get to know any of those details," I tell him, pressing Tim back into his seat before he has an aneurism. "You didn't show up for Ty's junior league games, you didn't pay the bills while Tim was in college working full time to support us, so you don't get to know about the ways we turned out happy despite all that." I'm just getting started now. "I fucking know you've read about me in the paper, too, and I don't care. Do you know I looked into giving you my liver? What the fuck was I thinking? You don't care enough about your own sons to get healthy, work on your grief, and be part of this family. Let me give you some parting comfort: we turned out ok. All of us. And it had nothing to do with you."

Tim and Ty just stare at me, and our father starts crying then. He buries his head in his hands and sobs and Tim pulls us all out into the hallway. "Enough," Tim says. "Let's get out of here. We've said our piece. Now let's let it lie." I exhale, feeling the weight of the years lifting a little bit. We start walking toward the elevator, but a nurse comes jogging down, calling out, "Stags? Are you Ted Stag's sons?"

Thirty-Nine
EMMA

I call Thatcher one last time before getting ready for my father's fundraiser. The call goes directly to voicemail, so he either has had his phone off for four days or he's declining my calls. I sigh. This was supposed to be simple. Hang out with him and his family a few times to get an interview. Get some great clips for my portfolio, and maybe earn some credibility at work. Why does it feel so shitty now that all of that has happened? I wonder what his family thinks about our apparent breakup. He must have told them he can't trust me...

I slide into my cocktail dress. It's a black shift, so it's more form-fitting than I prefer, but I like how the boat neck shows off my collar bones. Nicole insists the dress makes my boobs look hot, and I turn sideways, observing that they do look pretty high and front with this bra she made me buy. I fasten a string of pearls around my neck, but refuse to put on nylons in the middle of July.

As I pull my hair from the hot rollers, I think about how my end of the bargain worked out. Work has been amazing. Phil praised me during the staff meeting today, and my in-depth piece about the organ donors is going to be phenomenal. None of that feels as good as Thatcher making me a new coffee pot when I broke mine, or letting me have the ham sandwich even though it's both of our favorite.

I can't even look around my bedroom without remembering the feel of him taking me from behind. Every other man I've ever been with has treated me so cautiously, I felt like they didn't even respect that I'm a whole person. Thatcher managed to be wild, all the while focusing on what made me feel good. "He made you a neuron before he knew that mattered," I say to myself in the mirror. I try not to cry because I've put a touch of brown mascara on my auburn lashes and I don't want it to smudge.

I decide this is as good as I'm going to look, and I slip into a pair of heels, grab my bag, and begin my walk to the museum a few blocks away.

When I get there, I see Veronica first, sipping white wine and clinging to Logan's shoulder in such a way that her diamond ring is visible to everyone. "You're going to cut me with that," I tell her as she pulls me in for a fake hug and a fake cheek kiss. "Since when are we French?"

Veronica pouts at me and says, "Jesus, Emma, can you just behave one time for Dad?" Logan smirks and I roll my eyes, looking around for our mother.

I hear her before I see her. She's bellowing, "Oh *there's* our other daughter, Emma! Emma, you simply must meet Tristan Cummings!" I turn around just in time to be thrust toward a

Lainey Davis

smarmy-looking guy who is escorting my mother across the room. *Shit, she's trying to set me up,* I think, realizing this is how she is responding to her horror at learning I am engaged to Thatcher Stag. Was engaged? Anyway, there's no way I'm hanging out with this guy. She makes a face at me and I stick out a hand for Tristan to shake. "Tristan just made partner at his law firm," she says, fanning herself. "He's not even 30!"

"Congratulations," I say, smiling my fakest smile.

"What do you say we grab a drink to celebrate?" He asks and he honest-to-God winks at me.

"Hm, you know, I haven't said hello to my father yet," I tell him. "Won't you please excuse me?"

I never thought I'd be using my father as an excuse for, well, anything, but to escape Winky Lawyer, I slip toward the center of the gallery space. "Daddy," I say, coolly. "This is a lovely event."

"Emma!" He kisses my cheek. "You remember Mayor Gil."

I nod. I've actually interviewed him more than a few times, and printed critical articles about his proposed referendums. His smile is strained and he looks for something to say, so he gestures to the art I haven't had a chance to take in yet. "Interesting stuff, this."

As soon as I look up I know it's Thatcher's work. There's a glass woman in the middle of the room, the focal point of the entire gallery. She's made from orange and red glass, twisting

Fragile Illusion

up, lit from within. She's reaching toward the heavens, rays of red and orange and yellow shooting from her hands. The display is stunning. She's set on a pedestal, surrounded by low sculptures blown in vibrant greens and blues. She looks like the sun, rising from the sea. Triumphant. I nearly cry, the piece is so moving. I can't believe how the light and the space all work together to transform the work from what I saw on the shelves in his studio. I hear my father saying, "Yes, it's quite dramatic. Evidently the artist will be here tonight."

I gasp. *Thatcher will be here.* I start to look around, and I feel my mother come up and put her arm around me. "Emma, do you see what I meant about quality artwork? This piece here--this is the work of someone refined and elegant. Passionate and bold!"

I stare at her, not believing that she hasn't bothered to read the plaque bearing Thatcher's name. I don't really get time to ponder this for long, because Tristan glides back over holding two flutes of champagne. "Emma, darling," he says, his voice slick as an oil spill. "How about we take that drink now?"

I sense Thatcher arriving behind me and my body yearns for him. Then I hear his deep voice, smooth and certain, with an edge of danger. "The lady doesn't drink alcohol." I smell him, the familiar, wonderful scent of *him* above the evergreen soap. I feel his big, strong hand wrap around my waist and he pulls me close. I exhale, feeling like I haven't drawn a breath since our fight Sunday. When I look up at him, I'm stunned. Thatcher has trimmed his beard short and neat. He's cut his long hair underneath, buzzed it into a tight undercut and kept the top long. In his dark, fitted button-down shirt and black slacks, he looks so fucking sexy I nearly swoon. I let myself lean back against him, savoring the close warmth of his touch.

Tristan's expression darkens and he asks, "And just who might you be?"

I can feel Thatcher smile behind me. "Thatcher Stag," he says, sticking out one hand for a shake and keeping the other possessively on my stomach. "Emma's fiancé."

My mother giggles, a high-pitched, nervous sound, as my father's eyes start to bulge from his head. "How silly of me to forget to make introductions. This is just all so *new* that we aren't yet used to Emma's...betrothal."

My father clears his throat. "Yes, we're all quite excited. But if you'll excuse us, we are due to meet with the artist before things kick off this evening, so..." He drifts off and looks back and forth between Thatcher and the Mayor. I blush and bite my lower lip.

Thatcher clears his throat and keeps his hand out. "So glad you're enjoying my art, Mr. Cheswick. Pleased to meet you in person, Mr. Mayor. When I did a piece for the lobby of the city council building last spring, I only met with your staff."

Fragile Illusion

The mayor pumps Thatcher's hand. "Stag! Yes! Of course! I see the similarity in style with this work here. You did that black and gold bridge for us. We get so many compliments." He gestures toward my father with his drink. "Cheswick, you didn't tell me your daughter was marrying a *Stag*."

My mother's skin has gone grey and she starts fanning herself with her program. Veronica floats over with Logan and tries to ease the tension. "Can you tell us what inspired this piece here?" She leans in to read the plaque. "Emma? Oh! It's called Emma! That's you!"

Thatcher grins. He leans forward and beckons for my family and the mayor to lean in. He whispers as my father takes a sip of his gin. "I made this one the first time I saw your daughter naked."

Forty
THATCHER

Emma's dad spits gin all over the mayor and her mother screams. Chaos erupts, with staff members rushing over to dab up the mayor and wait staff offering everyone ice water. I just stand there, holding Emma against my body, enjoying the feel of her shaking gently, trying not to laugh. I found out who this event was for, and knew she would be here. Hell, I wanted to just skip the whole thing rather than deal with any drama. Maria, of course, practically dragged me here. I had intended to avoid Emma all night, but when I saw her walk in wearing that dress I just about came in my pants.

Then I saw her talking to that douchebag and I realized something huge. I don't want anyone else to be with Emma, because I want to be with Emma. I don't just want to sleep with her. I want to make her smile, and watch her get excited about researching weird, morbid articles. I don't want her going to fundraisers with uptight men who use too much gel. I want her with me, even if that means figuring out how to talk about my feelings and being in a fucking relationship. And realizing that makes my dick even harder than it was before.

I thrust my hips against Emma's back, letting her know just what's going on with me, and she inhales sharply. "Yes, Chezz," I whisper into her ear. "I want you right fucking now."

Fragile Illusion

She looks over her shoulder, and then back to her family. Her mother and sister are dabbing the mayor with napkins and apologizing while her father puts on a fake smile and tries talking to the guests who have pulled in closer to see what's going on. Nobody is going to notice our absence for a long time, and I grab Emma's hand, pulling her down the hall to the bathroom.

Outside the door, she grabs the wall. "Wait," she says, shaking her head. "No."

"Chezz," I say, nuzzling her neck, "I need you."

She flicks my chest and backs away from me. "You were such a dick the last time we talked, Thatcher, and now I haven't heard a word from you all week."

I sigh. "I know, Emma. I know. Please understand that this whole week? This whole month, really, has been so hard for me." I try to close the distance between us, needing to be close to her. "I don't know how to do all this," I say, waving my hand between us as she scowls at me. "But I'd love it if you could give me a chance to try."

Her face softens. "What do you mean? Try what, Thatcher?"

I pull her pale wrist to my lips and kiss her softly, stalling while I try to think of what I need to say. It all sounds so lame when I think about telling her everything on my mind. I look into her green eyes and see trust there, behind her frustration.

I shrug. "Just try to be better at talking to you. I don't want to push you away anymore. I want to be right by your side, even if you're puking in my brother's yard. I want to fight with you and bring you sandwiches. Be with you."

She crosses her arms and frowns. "You want to be with me? Like for 3 more days?"

I shake my head. "No. I mean yes, but I don't want to stop on Saturday. Emma." I touch her cheek. "I want all of you." I gesture over to her family. "All of that."

Emma licks her lips and runs her fingers along my collar. I breathe a sigh of relief, because I think I have won her back over. "All of this?" she asks, stretching up on tiptoes and biting my lower lip. I grin at her and kick open the bathroom door, tugging her in alongside me.

Once we're inside, I twist the lock and pull her in, sinking my lips against hers. I moan because it feels so god-damned good to taste her again. I delve into the corners of her mouth with my tongue, needing to claim her, to show her all the things I can't find words to say. She emits a tiny moan and I'm done for. I spin her around, looking over her shoulder at our reflection in the mirror as I pull her in to my chest. My hands splay over her tits, feeling her nipples spring to life under that tight-ass dress, and I slide one hand up to fist her hair. She has it all curly and draped over one shoulder and it looks hot as fuck.

Fragile Illusion

I tug on her hair, tilting her face up toward mine. "Emma," I whisper, my lips against her mouth. "Look how good we look together." She moans as I move my hand to her skirt, inching up the hem until I can slide a hand around to her wet heat. "You're so wet, Chezz," I say, nipping at her ear, watching her reflection in the mirror.

Emma leans forward, supporting her weight on the counter as I yank down her panties. She bites her lower lip and turns to look at me directly. "I can't believe we're doing this, Thatcher! In the bathroom at the Warhol..."

"Believe it, Emma." I drop a kiss on her mouth and pull one of her hands to my crotch. I help her ease down my fly and when she hoists my dick out of my pants I grunt like a wild animal. That's how she makes me feel--feral. I suck on Emma's neck and nudge her thighs apart with my knee as I palm my shaft. She's panting for me, and when I slide a finger along her pussy, I feel that she's swollen and wet. "You ready, Em?"

I line my tip up to her opening, teasing her folds and sliding along her wet seam. "Mmm, Thatcher, please. Now," she says, jutting her hips back against me, drawing me inside. I grin into the mirror and thrust inside, sliding home. Something snaps inside me, and I think about how this is the only place I want to be. The only woman I want by my side,

Lainey Davis

around my cock...everything. "Thatcher," she says, her voice snapping me back to the present.

Emma is slamming her hips back against me, bracing her arms against the sink and moaning. I match her rhythm and the sound of our skin slapping together echoes off the bathroom walls. I'm not going to last. It's been too long since I was with her, and I got too worked up seeing her talk to that asshole. "Chezz," I pant.

She nods. "I'm close, Thatcher. Oh! God, yes. Just like that." Her head drops back against my chest and I pull her tight, wrapping both arms around her body and rocking into her.

"Emma!" Her name is a plea, a prayer, a release, and I feel her contracting around me, coming right with me as I pour into her until I'm spent and replenished, empty and somehow bursting all at once.

Fragile Illusion

Forty-One
EMMA

I grasp the edge of the sink with both hands, trying to catch my breath as Thatcher pulls out. He sinks to his knees and, looking at me in the mirror, slowly eases my panties back up my legs, then adjusts my skirt.

He stands and washes his hands while I'm still trying to breathe slowly. Once I feel ready to adjust my hair and my bra, I notice that he's all tucked in and looking perfect. "When did you cut your hair," is all I can think to say. Every single time with that man leaves me dizzy, literally seeing stars and weak in the knees.

Thatcher runs a hand up the dark stubble of his under-cut. "You like it? I only went this short for Ty's wedding, because he asked nicely." He grins. And then I'm so overcome, I just start to cry. "Hey," he says, "Chezz, don't cry." He pulls me in and holds me. And he just feels so warm and safe that I actually do stop crying, believing for a moment that things can be ok.

"Can I tell you something?" he breathes into my hair and I nod against his chest. We always seem to communicate better when we're either naked or not looking at one another. He takes a deep breath and tells me, "My dad agreed to go to rehab."

Lainey Davis   219

I draw back so I can see his face, feeling like I have to look into his eyes for something like this. "He did? Truly?"

Thatcher nods, and tells me that the three of them had gone to see Ted in the hospital, spewed decades of angry words, and then made to leave until a nurse flagged them down. "He's going to give it a shot. His doctor said they can prescribe an antidepressant for him..."

He drifts off, and a tear leaks from my eye, because I know what it means for him to be telling me this, for him to finally be finding some closure in this area of his life. "Thatcher," I whisper. "I'm so glad for your family." And then I bury my face in his chest again, not wanting to let him go.

He holds me, murmuring into my hair about how he and his brothers are going to sign up for a group at the hospital. They have programs there for grieving lost parents, and the Stag brothers never really worked on their feelings about losing their mom.

"Hey," I tell him, reaching up to cup his face. I smile and look into his eyes, wanting so badly for his return smile to be mine for always. "I'm really proud of you."

He shakes his head. "No, Emma. It's because of you. You led me to find him, and you pressed me to be honest with my brothers. This never would have happened without you. So thank you, Chezz." He kisses my palm. "Thank you." And then his lips are on mine and nothing else matters.

Fragile Illusion

Until I hear someone pounding on the bathroom door.

"Emma Cheswick, you open that door this instant." It's my mother. "I know you're in there."

I sigh and look up at Thatcher, who adjusts his collar and runs a hand through what's left of his long hair. "You ready for this?" I ask him, and he nods.

When I open the door, my mother digs her nails into my arm and pulls me into the hall. "How. Could. You. Humiliate. Us. Like. This?" She jabs an index finger into my chest with each word.

Ordinarily I would be super stressed out to see her freaking out like this, but I'm still high on a Stag orgasm, and I'm strangely calm. So I tell her, "Excuse me, mother, but I think I am the one who should be embarrassed." She recoils. "You've been nothing but rude to Thatcher since you met him in the hospital. You treat him like garbage and make assumptions on him based on his appearance, which I love by the way, and then you don't even do your diligence to look at the fucking name of the artist in the space where Dad's having a fundraiser."

Thatcher squeezes my shoulder supportively while my mother flares her nostrils. I keep going. "And further, I should be embarrassed that you're so hung up on appearances that you kept me with a useless doctor for years of uncontrolled seizures. Thatcher has been super supportive, helping me with my new medications from Dr. Khalsa. You haven't even asked about my visit from last week."

I want to walk away. I'm feeling absolutely done with her. But I'm not expecting her to start crying.

Tears roll down her face, smearing her foundation. "Emma," she whispers as Veronica approaches. "I was so scared." She sinks into a folding chair that's been stashed in the hallway. "Do you know what it's like when your baby has something wrong? I don't mean what other people think, although I worried about that, too." She dabs at her face with a tissue. "I mean the feeling of utter helplessness. I couldn't help you. I took you to the doctor everyone talked about. I didn't know there were other ideas, newer treatments. I just thought that was going to be it for you, and I needed to keep you isolated and safe."

She looks up between me and Thatcher and Veronica, now. Everyone is silent as she pleads with us. "I thought I was doing my best by you, and then when I realized how out-dated it all was, how much *better* you were doing with a doctor you'd found on your own..." She drifts off and swallows. I can see her struggling to breathe in between sobs and I just stand there, my hand on Thatcher's on my shoulder. I need the warm touch of his skin to keep me grounded.

"I was dreadfully ashamed, Emma. Of the years I cost you. I'm so terribly sorry, and I don't know how to begin to make amends for that."

The hallway is silent for a long time until Veronica sniffles. I bite my lip. "I accept your apology," I whisper, and then, for the first time in a very long time, I lean forward and willingly embrace my mother.

Forty-Two
THATCHER

Shit got really real there at the Andy Warhol museum tonight, and I feel like I need a good, stiff drink. Except I'm leaving with Emma on my arm, and she doesn't drink alcohol. She and the other Cheswicks cried and hugged for awhile. Eventually her dad shook my hand and told me my sculpture was nice. I try to imagine how I'd react if some asshole told me he made art from my naked daughter, and I decide Mr. Chezz isn't all that bad.

Emma wants to walk home, so I take her high heels from her, draping an arm over her shoulders while she walks barefoot along the sidewalk. "Did you really make that sculpture based on me?" she says, the street light reflecting off her green eyes and looking amazing. It gives me ideas. She's always inspiring my work, and I love that.

I nod. "You looked like the dawn after a long darkness, naked and glowing. Aurora," I tell her. "I don't ever want to forget that moment." We walk in silence a bit more until I gather up the nerve to tell her what I really need to say. "Emma," I say, squeezing her hand. "I want to talk about us."

"Hm?" she looks down, stepping over a pothole as we cross the street. I squeeze her shoulder and stop walking.

Fragile Illusion

"Chezz, I don't want to end things with you after the wedding this weekend."

Her eyes dance back and forth, her gaze searching mine. "I need you in my life to keep calm in emergencies. You inspire me, Emma. Christ, do you know what you do for my work?" I gesture around. "All of that back there, that's you. That's all you. You are my muse." She starts crying now, and I rub my thumb on her cheeks, brushing away the tears. "Be with me, Chezz. Give us a shot." There's an eternity where my heart stops and she doesn't respond, and I think I've put myself fully on the line, raw and exposed, and she's going to turn me down. But then she closes her eyes and stretches up, grabs hold of my face with both hands, and sinks into the sweetest, best kiss of my life. Then I know she's mine.

Forty-Three
EMMA

Nicole insists on giving me a ride to Ty and Juniper's wedding. Thatcher had to be there super early to deal with flowers and tuxes and stuff, but promised he'd come outside to see if Nicole approves of him.

She spends an hour setting my hair in hot rollers in the morning, spraying my red locks into a cascading fountain of curls. "You look hot as fuck," she tells me as I slip into a pair of jade green strappy heels. They match the dress perfectly, and I twirl around, watching the skirt billow out. I definitely look ready for a celebrity wedding.

Ty and Juniper are getting married in the conservatory, surrounded by Thatcher's glass of course, and because Ty and his teammates will all be there, security is heightened for the whole area. Nicole beams as we pull up to the guard blocking the street from through traffic. "I feel like I'm chauffeur for the rich and famous," she tells me. Then she leans out the window and tells the guard, "I'm delivering Emma fucking Cheswick to Thatcher Stag."

He looks through the window over the top of his sunglasses and waves Nicole on. She squeals. "Nick, you're being ridiculous," I tell her. "They're just *people.*"

But I feel giddy when I spy Thatcher up ahead, waiting for me on the sidewalk. Nicole whistles and I don't blame her. Thatcher in a tux is pure elegance, pure sex, and all mine. He grins as we pull up, running a hand through his neatly-trimmed beard. He opens a door for me and whistles as I climb out. Nicole laughs, but Thatcher looks awestruck. "Chezz," he says. "You look so beautiful right now." His words are so earnest that I blush and squeeze his hand. "You ready for all this," he asks, gesturing toward the photographers swarming around the Escalades and Range Rovers bearing Fury players and their dates.

Nicole sighs and clutches her hands under her chin. Then she leans over and sticks out her hand toward Thatcher. "Nicole Thomas, best friend. Damn glad to meet you, Thatcher Stag." He grins at her, shaking her hand. "You take care of our girl, now."

He pulls me against his side and kisses the top of my head. "She doesn't need taking care of, Nicole. I need her to take care of *me*."

When Thatcher says that, Nicole punches her horn and gives me a double thumbs up. "Emma, he's a keeper. Go mingle with the hockey stars, get me someone's number, and then go have hot sex and beautiful babies." I laugh as she peels out.

Thatcher escorts me inside, where the entire conservatory seems to be in bloom to celebrate Juniper and Tyrion. Thatcher kisses my hand and leaves me with some other guests while he takes his place up front just as Tim and Ty enter the room. The trio of brothers standing tall, dressed to kill, is quite a sight to behold. I hear a sniffle beside me and see Anna Stag taking pictures of her grandsons, then dabbing her eyes with a hanky.

I give her leg a squeeze just as the violins start playing and Juniper makes her way toward her beloved. Tall and sleek in a simple, elegant white dress, Juniper has eyes only for Ty. They make their way through the ceremony, holding hands. Ordinarily I find this kind of thing cheesy, but I can't help but smile during the vows when Juniper blurts out, "I'm keeping my name!"

Ty smiles at her and squeezes her hands. He says, "I sort of thought you might, Junebug." When he leans in to kiss her, Thatcher pulls him back, scolding him for jumping the gun.

After they are pronounced married, there's a loud commotion from the crowd of well-wishers. I bite my hand in glee when I see all Juniper's rowing friends line one side of the aisle holding oars. Ty's teammates line the other side of the aisle holding hockey sticks. The two sides form an unlikely arch, and Ty and Juniper walk through their friends,

Fragile Illusion

laughing. Smiling. Happy and in love. I catch Thatcher's eye and we share a moment until he walks forward.

He kisses his grandmother's cheek and then, with a lustful look, squeezes my shoulder and asks, "Gram, can you excuse Emma for a minute? I need her." Anna Stag smiles and pats my hand as Thatcher tugs me into the hall.

"Where are we going," I ask, looking around, until I realize we are in the hall where we first met. Where he took me for nefarious purposes. Things have certainly changed in the past month. "Oh," I say, running my hands down his chest. Ty picked out stunning grey tuxes to match his brothers' eyes and I let my fingers trail down the long tie, wrapping it in my fist and pulling Thatcher in for a kiss.

He growls and boxes me in against the wall like he did that first night, nibbling my neck, and this time, I let him. Eagerly. "Emma," he breathes, "Do you want to know what I was thinking about during that ceremony?"

I roll my head to the side as he kisses a trail up to my ear, down along my chin. He smells so good and I love these gentle touches. "How much your brother loves your new sister-in-law?" I ask him, playfully.

He shakes his head and looks into my eyes. "No, Emma. I was thinking about you. How right you look sitting with my family, being here for my family's important days. I love you, Emma Cheswick."

I feel a whoosh as my breath leaves my body. Oh, to hear these words from this man! Since he asked me to be with him the other night, he's been so present. We've barely spent a moment apart in all that time, and now, as I lean against the glass wall of the conservatory where we met, I know I feel the same. "I love you, too, Thatcher."

Epilogue
Six Months Later
THATCHER

"Just try your best to relax," Emma says, standing behind the couch and rubbing my shoulders. I have restless legs and can't settle my hands. This day is so intense. I look around the industrial loft we just renovated so Emma and I could finally move in together. I found a fantastic building in Emma's neighborhood that met all our needs--she can still walk to work, I have a studio for my furnace and kilns, and we have lots of space for her to set up a home office.

Emma slides open one of the glass panels I made to separate different areas of the loft. In doing so, she lets in more light and I can see how hard she's worked to set things up for today. "You bought more chairs?" I ask, noticing that she's arranging comfortable seats around small tables with fresh flowers. Emma nods and dusts off her hands.

"I think we're ready. Alice should be here soon with all the food." I nod and Emma kisses my cheek just as we hear the groaning sound of the old elevator bringing up my siblings. Tim and Ty look about as relaxed as me, which is to say they're stiff and sort of grey.

Today, we're going to introduce our father to our families. Throughout his time in rehab, he leveled out his antidepressant medication and went through intensive therapy to both face his grief and begin atoning for his choices. We all started receiving packages--birthday and Christmas cards to symbolize all those holidays he missed since our mother died. Letters expressing his regret that he missed all of our important milestones by allowing his grief be more important than our needs. We don't know if his liver has recovered enough to keep him healthy, but he's been sober for six months and we all agreed to have him over after we met with him a few times at his rehab. It's been hard emotionally, but I've had Emma by my side the whole time.

Living with her really feels as seamless as breathing. Suddenly I had someone to come home to every night, an inspiration for my work, someone to collaborate with for ideas and challenges. I always thought it would be so much work for little reward to give myself to a woman, but Emma is my partner in every way. Hell, she's in the middle of a huge investigative story, but she set aside time this weekend to support me and my family. She reminds me every day that she's not going anywhere, and I trust her. I love the hell out of her, and I can see that she loves me right back.

Petey squirms out of Tim's arms and runs over and climbs in my lap. I hold him tight, rubbing his warm, sticky cheek against my own. Normally we have all our family dinners at Tim and Alice's place, but everyone agreed it was better to

Fragile Illusion

have this first meeting at a more neutral space. I sigh and stand, slinging Petey up onto my shoulders. I hear the elevator start to move again, and my breath catches in my chest.

Emma reaches up on tip-toe to kiss my cheek and squeezes my hand. "You can do hard things, Thatcher Stag," she says, looking into my eyes with those emerald orbs of hers. "I'm right here by your side and I love you."

"I love you, too, Chezz," I say. And knowing that helps me feel strong.

When she opens the door to my father, she isn't awkward or timid. She pulls him in for a quick hug and says, "Ted, hi. I'm Emma Cheswick, Thatcher's fiancé. We're so glad to have you here in our home."

THE END

Thank you so much for reading!

Would you consider leaving me a review?

Can't get enough Stag Brothers?

Follow me on Facebook
(www.facebook.com/LaineyDavisWriter)
or subscribe to my newsletter (http://eepurl.com/dvDKzH)
so you never miss a new release.

~~Lainey